This book has been written from som
my past life, it is set in the late eightie
comments were accepted and humor
Please do not be offended if you do n
my sense of humour or language.
If you think this book is about you then it probably is.
Feel complimented you have made a difference in my life.

All names in the book are purely coincidental and are not particularly aimed at anyone.

I would like to dedicate this book to my kids, my other kids, and an Angel in my life.

There I was showing my one-way ticket to the ticket inspector to be stamped and approved as well as supping a disgustingly pale but wet and warm plastic cup of British rail tea that I would have said tasted like cat pea, had I ever tasted cat pea to know the taste.

"Change at Birmingham for Reading," The inspector said as he gave me my ticket back, which I took with my right hand. My left hand was busy juggling the brew in a clown juggling act fashion in an attempt not to spill it and burn my hand again.

I don't think they had an independent suspension system fitted to this model locomotive, that system only came as standard in Nineteen eighty-seven and you could feel every bump in the train track.

Fifth August 1986 and I'm stuck in a train squashed in next to an overweight slob who should have bought two seated tickets for himself as he took up that amount of space, on my way to Aldershot, the basic training depot of the Parachute regiment for twenty-six weeks of voluntary mental hardship, physical beasting and short haircuts.

The train arrived at Stoke on Trent, the big person next to me struggled himself to get up and proceeded to get off the train, (I'm sure I saw the train lift when he got off). A few minutes later another fella sat next to me who was slim but about 10 feet tall, the train must have been full.

I was hoping to have a peaceful journey down from Chorley, no chance. About 5 minutes later the tall man spoke to me and said words to the effect of how ya doin? After clearing my throat of the cat pea that was left, I looked up about a foot and replied,

"Eye, not bad, how are you? How far ya going?"

In a slightly twanged Irish accent, I just about managed to understand him saying,

"I'm gan to Exeter for a short while".

In the interests of being polite I asked if he had relatives down there or was it a holiday.

"Neither, I'm on my way to a place called Lympstone for 5 months. It's the Commando training centre, Royal Marines. I've come over from Belfast to get out of there. It's the only way forward, I'm twenty-eight now I've got to do this before I'm 30. After that, I'll be too bloody old, and the body can only take so much stick. I've already served in the Royal Irish Rangers, so I know a bit of what's going to happen, and I have a ten-year-old daughter and a hungry wife to feed.   'How about you, how far are you going?'

"Well I've just left a good job to do similar to you but I'm going airborne, I'm off to Aldershot, the Para's. I think I'd much rather do the Marines thing but it's too late now I'm half way there,   but most of all I can't join the Marines because my moustache doesn't grow past the ends of my mouth for some strange reason, so it makes me look like Hitler, I wouldn't fit in".

He introduced himself as Conall O Leary. The conversation went on for about an hour and I almost missed that we had stopped at my change over town- Birmingham. We said our good byes and good lucks, and both thought that we wouldn't see each other again.

I got off the train and walked past several groups of people congregating on the platform,   there were punk rockers with pink and red Mohican hair, chains, padlocks and huge safety pins dangled from all over their clothes.

They sported holes in their jeans and patches made of cloth beer mats were sewed to the back of their jackets. Every one of the punks smoked and they all had spotty mouths and noses probably brought on by excessive solvent abuse.

The next group of people were very interesting because although there were two different sexes you could only just tell them apart. All the young men wore eye shadow, blusher and lippy and had 6-foot-wide shoulder pads which I think made them look like Sue Ellen from Dallas, half of the group had leg warmers around their ankles.

One of the young girls had a perm like Whitney Houston had at that time. One of the most noticeable boys, who was wearing girls high heel shoes with what looked like three quarter length chino pants, had flattened his hair on one side of his head and had a side parting which took the rest of his hair right across his face covering one eye and down past his nose and mouth. All to be seen of his face was a very pink make up coloured cheek, a dangly ear ring, and a well decorated eyelash with matching shadow, a proper new romantic Phil Oakey-ite.

I knew I was approaching the right platform; all I had to do now was pass the last group of people, majority black or what you might call Rastafarian. They wore the most colourful coats I have ever seen, and they were jamming to some reggae master on their over inflated portable boogie box. I didn't recognise the music but thought it very cool.

I stepped onto the next train sat down and whilst waiting for the next ticket inspector looked through the window and witnessed two police officers being attacked by three or four bikers with long hair and leathers and a group of police colleagues racing to the rescue from the other end of the platform. It all happens on the train I thought.

The train set off and several miles on we temporarily stopped at a red light. I didn't want to risk another cup of cat pea, so I tried to get to sleep, only to be interrupted by the ticket inspector. I must have dozed off again as the trains arrival at Aldershot came as a surprise! I quickly found the bus that would take me on the final leg of my journey to my new home for a few months, the Parachute Regiment Training Centre Aldershot.

I was met by what I thought was a Corporal or at least he had two stripes on his arm and directed me to stand with about 30 others. He addressed us all in loudly.

"Right you lot, get yourselves down to that building over there, it's got C-company splatted all over it, you can't miss it, get in, get a room, put your kit in a locker and then get yourselves outside."

Ten minutes later, we were mostly all outside hands in pockets talking amongst ourselves introducing ourselves and dossing about, thinking this doesn't seem that bad after all.

"You 'orrible bunch of miscreants, get down and give me 50, go on, get down, press ups, proper ones" shouted a voice from a group of three soldiers who wore the coveted wings on their arms of their disruptive pattern military smocks. The one that shouted the command quickly walked towards us, continually shouting at us to do proper press ups. The other two verbally abused all of us, picking each comment to match each individual and his looks. For a split second, I looked up and accidentally caught the eye of what must have been the drill sergeant. I guessed this because he had a pace stick under his arm and three stripes on his arm, and he shouted back at me with a deep croaky whisky poisoned voice.

"Get your curly head down toward the floor Shirley temple, how dare you even think of looking at me you horrible piece of nothing".
I could see concrete but could still hear the sergeant blast an order out to his corporal.

"Corporal Camilari, I want this piece of nothings hair cut first, down to the bone as it should be do you hear?"
"Yes, Sergeant Hunter first in the queue"

I thought to myself 'maybe I should have cut my hair before I came.'

We didn't even finish our press ups, it was embarrassing that we only managed on average about 15 each, when we were told to stand up and run on the spot. One of the corporals explained that we were here as 'volunteers' in Her Majesties elite parachute regiment. Of the 32 intake trainees, only 15 at best would pass out. Based on the miserable press up performance, 15 would more likely be eight.

"Carry on running and follow me".

We were all doubled away to the company stores where each recruit was issued with several items of kit including socks, underwear, waterproofs, all in dpm green, and three pairs of boots, black. I heard someone say in a broad Liverpudlian accent

"Christ I've never had as many clothes, when do we get the guns "?

I'm sure he was talking to his mate who was also a scouser as the other recruit gave an approving nod and man giggle. We picked our stuff up and quickly shoved it in the cloth kit bag that we were supplied with which was of course olive drab green. Corporal Camilari rattled out the command.

"get your 'orrible little arses outside now"

Everybody picked up their kit and with difficulty made way or scrambled through and up the narrow passage way up the six steps up to the outside ground where the two corporals were waiting.

By this time just about everybody had a sweat about them. The hot weather wasn't helping, it was August and a guestimate at the temperature would be about twenty-three to twenty-eight degrees. I had a quick look around at the recruits and everyone was puffing and panting and looking at each other in disbelief. I could see their thoughts in their eyes. What have we let ourselves in for? The other corporal who I thought was quiet up to now spoke but did not shout with a very authoritative voice.

"Fall in! Two ranks. If you leave any kit behind you will pay for it; put your kit bags on your backs, running on the spot, right turn".

About three of the thirty-two recruits turned left; fortunately, I wasn't one of them,

"Army right you prick's", Corporal Camilari shouted. Within five minutes, we were in our barrack room trying to set our stall in the small space that we had. A bed, a cupboard, a shelf and a space to put a picture of your loved one, or if your loved one was Sam fox, then there was a space for her.

We all managed to introduce ourselves to each other of a fashion, I kept forgetting all the names so ended up like everybody else with using nicknames, like Taff, Scouse, Geordie, Jock, and there was a bloke called Miller who for some unknown reason was of course nicknamed Windy. Oh, and Andy white was to be known as Chalky, complete puzzlement to me!

Moments later, amongst the boyish laughter and foul language, we were disturbed and summoned to appear outside in PT kit. Lightweight green trousers (to be known as lightweights) with elastics as supplied rolled over at the top of the pussers boot so as not to be made to look scruffy – apparently.   A white t-shirt with a V-neck, looking very uncool and far too regimented.

With a very brief description of basic drill and line forming, we were marched towards the north corner of the parade ground where there was a Porto cabin. There was a man sat down on a fold away director's chair, smoking a fag, wearing a white doctors type overcoat, what on earth was this?

We were all halted and made to stand to attention; we waited in silence for what seemed like hours but were in fact seven and a half minutes, as that was the time it took for the squaddies barber to get ready.

"Right Shirley Temple, get your girly head in there and come out looking like a proper soldier"

My eyes shut tight when I saw the electric hair cutter with its number one attachment, projected at my forehead like a well-aimed torpedo from a battleship. There was no mirror inside the Porto cabin, just a man with some electric blades, no requests, no short back and sides or flat tops, side partings, just a number one.

At least we didn't have to pay for it.

I walked out stroking my bald head and listened to the comments from the rest of the recruits and tried to make a joke of it, picked up my kit bag and re-joined the squad. The corporal told me to make my way to the barrack room and finish off getting organised as there was a

[9]

briefing soon. One by one, the bald heads came into the barracks swearing and cursing the fact they had lost their locks choice or no, all for the love of the Queens shilling, Yeah right!

The briefing ended up being a lesson in ironing and personal hygiene so of course we were all bored by the "pay attention" statement that came from Corporal Camilari's mouth every five minutes. Little did we know that we would be tested, inspected and punished for any imperfections that were spotted on parade every morning at five thirty in the morning. Maybe we should have paid attention, as this would be the routine we would follow for several weeks.

By the fourth week of training, everybody was knackered. Polishing boots and ironing lightweights, cleaning the ablutions and getting ready for the next day. Preparation and planning prevent piss poor performance I think was the saying that everybody seemed to use, even when brushing your teeth.
Fortunately, I was in a room of only six and one of the lads had brought a tape player and just happened to have a Tubeway Army album, which he played once or twice. He was a Taff and I couldn't tell what he said when I asked him as a joke has he got any Kate Bush, so I presumed that he didn't.

As usual, half past five in the morning and we heard the two dustbin lids banging together outside and then inside the room. This wasn't Corporal Camilari's attempt at learning percussion, it was the roll call or reveille or a warning to let us know that we were about to be inspected so that required a last-minute dash around and hope for the best.

My turn came to shout attention as the staff came in the room and we all stood to attention at the foot of our beds, oh shit Sergeant Hunter was here as well, guess we won't get a weekend pass for a while. A weekend pass was only given if the instructors were happy. Sergeant Hunter looked in disgust and disbelief at one of the corporals and spoke with his whisky polluted voice

"Corporal what the fuck is the piece of shit doing underneath this piece of shits bed"?

He produced a tiny piece of fluff that had probably been there for years.

"I want this man's bed and kit outside in the bin area ready for inspection tonight at seven o clock sharp, if he wants live in shit then that's the place for him in the shithouse"

Sergeant continued his inspection of the room. At least three others were reprimanded with press ups and another had his bedding block thrown out the window because it wasn't regulation length and width. The Sergeant had a mark on his pace stick which was calibrated to the exact measurement of the bedding blanket and sheets folded up in a specific way to a specific shape.

I had to carry my kit out after scran and had to ask Taff Tubeway Army if he would give me a hand with the bed, then I had to sweep out all the bin area and mop it after removing the three steel bins.

I hanged my kit on hangers and placed them on the gaps in the open brick enclosure, which was about 10 foot by 10-foot square with two openings in it. I redid my bed block, finished off cleaning, and waited for yet another inspection. Surely, they can't expect me to sleep in here tonight.

It took me two hours to get everything back to where it belonged back in the barrack room, I think Corporal Camilari felt sorry for me; he just turned up and said
"Right weasel (my name was Wealan but he always came up with an equivalent which sounded similar) get your shit back in there at the double"

"Yes staff"

By the ninth week of training the physical side of it was getting more intense but more enjoyable, we had a good feeling when we were being beasted and everybody managed to encourage each other, but sometimes it wasn't enough as four more recruits had been back squaded through injury. This just meant they would join on one of the squads in the first or second week of training dependant on the severity of the injury and the length of time it took to recover. Those of us that were left felt more and more confident by the day.

One morning Sergeant Hunter and the two corporals arrived in a Bedford four tonner. The good old squaddie cab, it wasn't overfull with 13 of us. The back canopy was down so we could not see where we were going and we set off with webbing and full water bottle. What seemed like around an hour later, the Bedford stopped.

"Right out you get lads, let's be avin ya. Get out of the bus and split into four groups of three. The one odd man can be special and tag on to the best group, which ever that group is. Corporal Camilari double em down that track about one mile to meet captain Macintosh -you won't be able to miss him. He's in his own vehicle that damned camper van thing!"

"Right Sergeant, you heard! Two ranks double march, left right, left right, left right"

We were about half a mile away from the RV when I spotted a bright blue and white two-tone rectangular object with some camouflage foliage scrim cover over the top of it. A round, shiny chrome mirror protruded either side. It looked like some mad attempt to disguise it as an army vehicle, when in fact the effect was more like something out of a mobile home TV advert for the outdoor life. As we approached, I could see the nineteen sixty-seven VW campervan oversized side door fully open. Inside was the company commander, the Slazenger golf ball chewing Rupert Macintosh, just putting down this month's issue of Country Life (the quintessential magazine) on the foldaway VW table, next to his cup of Yorkshire tea.

"Corporal, tell me why, (a very quick time check happened), yes, why are you forty-three minutes late arriving here, when my instructions were specific. I wanted you here at 11.06, not 11.49, and I only brought six custard creams which are now all gone thank you very much! Stand the men at ease immediately."

"Right Sir sorry Sir. Listen in then, stand at ease".

We all looked at each other with disbelief. Is he taking the piss or has he really no custard creams left? Fifey, Taff Jones and I decided to join forces to confirm our suspicions on the biscuit subject and confront Corporal Camilari.

"Corporal does this mean we have come all this way to find there are no custard creams left?"

"Wozzalwil (another odd name for me, haven't heard that one before) get these maps and dish em out to the groups, I'm just getting grids now you prick! "

I took the maps off the corporal and attempted to fold them into some sort of readable, portable navigation accessory, and handed them out,

"Here Taff give that map to Jock Mernie will you he's good at tennis!"

Taff and I were looking around the bright vehicle in admiration and astonishment, when the Sandhurst trained yuppie wearing the number 2 parade shirt with the collar worn outside, on top of an immaculately pressed green and brown dpm smock, slightly resembling an abstract version of Elvis Presley and a 1970,s porn star, opened his mouth.

"Not bad is she, cost me £4k and it's not bad on fuel either, had it painted original colours and serviced it before I came out, sort of a recreational thing don't you know"

I almost ignored him but thought better of it when I realised he thought we were looking at the van,

"Oh, yes sir we were just in awe at the job you have done with that scrim net on top of the van, I bet you can't see it from above"

If in fact, somebody just happened to send up a spotter plane to see if there were any such objects lying around in the middle of the military training area. The Captain cleared his throat with almost embarrassment trying not to swallow the golf ball and replied.

"Yes, getting back to your field exercise, here are the grids you need. At each RV point there will be a Bergen (rucksack) with provisions and instructions inside. Take the Bergen with you; don't leave it, as you will need it later. The whole exercise should take 14 hours and six minutes. You will be tabbing forty-three miles in total and no fires until the second RV , which is fourteen miles from the extraction point for the PVR's (Premature Voluntary Release from the armed service) should there be any" he said with sincere sarcasm.

"Right men, off you trot"

Corporal Camalari led the groups away who were in stitches discussing the mentality, intelligence or lack of it, and university education that the officers of today, the leaders of men, and the upper echelon of society, the top brass that would take the country to war and back, had!

"Here Taff, let's have a look at that piece of bog paper that Rodney calls a map, let's see if we can't figure out where we are going"

[15]

Taff was one of those Welshman who decided to ask a question after everything everybody said then answer his own question himself and ask a question in a question he had already asked?

"Where are we going then, oh are we are going there are we? Are you using mag to grid system, are you?"

Then he would sometimes step forward in a karate stance with one foot forward and point at you waving his finger in annoyance and give you the answer himself,

"Yes, mag to grid that's what you do, don't you? Soon get there with that you will."

"Ok cheers Taff".

Corporal Camalari informed us that the exercise was to include camouflage and concealment, escape and evasion, survival and nutrition in the field, oh and we will be attacked by other forces, meaning other companies of paras who were more advanced in their training than us.

"Is that all corporal? No, it's raining! Bugger"

We were taken to the top of the nearest hill and then set free, well not exactly free but allowed to go off on our own following the grid references we were given by the whatsername in the camper van and expected to follow the instructions that were found along the route. Easy!

Half a mile down the way Taff disturbed the silence.

"Do we have to follow the map do we, I knows this place I do. We could take a short cut and end up at the Bergen, get the instructions and off to the next RV in half the time don't you know".

"What's that Taff?"

"Well I've been here before see, and I know that if we walk past that tree over there and up past the brow of the next hill where the six woolybacks are, I reckon that Bergen is about 457 feet away from the style on the nearside of the river."

"Bloody ell Taff, you can come again. Ere Jock, listen to this. Valley expert Taff reckons that at least an hour can be saved doing a diversion through there."

I pointed to the congregation of woolybacks grazing by the lone tree.
 "I reckon he's right, come on, we'll beat the rest of the groups who had already gone their separate ways hoping to succeed in their mission with flying colours.
"Taff is there anything else you've got hidden in that orient express of yours?"
 Which of course was a train there fore was cockney rhyming slang for brain, well I never was good at English!
We set off using the short cut and within about twenty minutes the Bergen was in sight sat upright in the middle of an arrangement of small rocks waiting to be taken. Pleased with our time saving plan, we closed the last steps to find the rucksack, opened it and emptied the contents on the floor. Two dead chickens, a packet of firelighters, some carrot's and some more grid references.
 "Well at least we can eat. Maybe it's a test of our obedience, that captain did say no fires till the second RV."
"Have we got more grids have we, ah there they are."
Taff took the map and studied it.
"Get on with it then Taff, "barked Jock Mernie, "about time we got the scran on, bloody starved I am."

"Err, well err, perhaps if we, err, just a minute, I'm just thinking. Erm, well if we, no wait yes if we go up there, follow the track to the right of the river, cross the river about one mile, pick up grid reference at the corner of the farmers field, walk along the ridge there, cross two fields and that should get us to the RV."

Jock Mernie and I exchanged glances, we were both starving! Decision made, I picked up the Bergen after filling it with our provisions and off we went. The conversation was lively moving from Maggie Thatcher to Sam Fox, Lisa Stansfield to Lloyd Cole and the Commotions, and then of course, back to women.

"Jock, are you still seeing that girl you were on about last night, where does she live Glasgow? I asked.

"Eye well up to now yeh, haven't seen her since she dropped me off at the train station to come down here, not sure if I will see her again. I've had sore bollocks since last time we had it, have you ever had the sore bollocks syndrome Weal's?"

"No not me pal, I've been ultra-careful where I put mine which means basically that I've not had as many conquests as you!"

"What about you Taff?" Jock Mernie asked.

All of a sudden, without answering the question about sexual diseases, Taff stepped forward and adopted his karate stance, thrusting one arm forward in the air in no particular direction with open hand. In a clear dramatic voice, he said,

"Papillion de mer,   Butterflies of love,   Crabs."

I fell to the ground laughing, inadvertently losing the Bergen, and spilling the contents everywhere. Jock lost a grip on his water canister which triple somersaulted and landed upside down in a pile of cowpat.

"Bloody ell Taff",

I managed while still laughing and holding my aching ribs,

"You never seem to disappoint with your witty one-liners."

"Ken, twitty one-liners, look where my water landed! Where did you manage to learn French anyway, were you in the foreign legion or summat?"

"Well now you mention it, no! I read a book on the subject I have, haven't I just."

"Do they have French books in Wales where you come from then, where ever that is?"

"Of course, they do and I come from Harlech in the north, get to the castle go down the hill turn right, half a mile turn left, and my family house in opposite the library."

"Not in the valleys then?" Jock said.

"No not in the valleys but not far off."

"What other useless books have you read then Taff, orienteering perhaps?"

"Well I was half way through the Principles of Psychology by Sigmund Freud just before I joined up you see, but I got bored of listening to the theory of the unconscious mind, I found the January's edition of Woman's Weekly more interesting didn't I."

"Woman's Weekly!" I protested,

"What on earth is the world coming to, even the Scottish don't read that do they Jock?"

"Don't get me going or I'll end up in hysterics again, then we'll never finish this exercise. Come on Taff, lead the way."

Soon enough there we were at the RV already unpacking the goodies from the Bergen. I started the bivvi fire that, with a bit of luck, would cook the chickens and carrots. Taff said he would go and have a word with the farmer who was in a tractor in the next field and see if he could get some spuds so we could have chicken casserole. I asked him not to forget the herbs. Jock was busy gathering local foliage which would be helpful in our camouflage and concealment and would be spread over the top of three drab olive-green ponchos tied together with green G10 stores supplied bungees, much the same as what Captain Macintosh did but on a smaller scale. Jock did a good job of the makeshift tent. There was no wind to put the fire out or put a chill on us and none of the light rain that came down got us wet, so we sat down and watched the chopped-up chicken cook on the fire and waited for Taff and his spuds to appear.

"Ay up Taff hurry up with them spuds,"

"I've got some new potatoes, mushrooms, leeks and some bread"

"Excellent chicken, mushroom, leek and carrot butties then"

I remarked,

"Can't wait"

The three of us managed three large chicken butties with raw carrots, but the leeks were used in the foliage, we then studied our next instructions.

The Ambush.

"Taff, I keep seeing things, are you playing tricks on me?"
"No what do ya mean seeing things"
"There it is again, just whipped around me head, like a star shaped Mars Bar"
"Eh"
"There it is again, now there is about six thousand little mice doing circles on the floor, oh my god what's happening,   my fingers have changed into several pairs of scissors,   and look you have grown a turnip on your head"
"What, Yer aff yer heid Mon, where's the drugs gimme some"

What on earth had happened, I could not control any thoughts or figure what was going on in front of me, my bodily functions seemed to disappear, and my vision had become a blurry mess, all that was in front of me were random mutating objects of my youth in very odd mixes of shapes.

"Taff, where were those mushrooms from"?
"Err, a patch o'r there. Why?
"Because my friend, you have given Wheeltrim the hallucinogenic's Mon   He's away with the fairies, look at the state of him he's well-spaced out, his fingers are pointing at airborne chocolate bars for god's sake, did you have any of em, "?
"Na, don't like mushrooms, did you have some"
"Nope, wish I had, any left?"
"Wheels are you ok lad?"
"Yeah man,   love all around man, peace and love all around, would you like a mini mars bar, or some mice man"
Taff looked at Jock for help

[21]

"Err Jock what's the cure for lunacy in the field "
"Beer, but as we have none, better just leave him to it"

Inside the package was a three-page mission, the idiots guide to an ambush along with what to do after the event and what to eat beforehand, which wasn't chicken and carrot butties, with magic mushrooms!

Half an hour passed, and the mice and mars bars had almost gone, but verbal gibberish resembling pig Latin still flowed from a dribbling mouth.

As we studied the grand plan we realised it was us that was to do the ambushing. What's more, it was our mates we were going to ambush. Ah well, at least we would be able to get one over on Fifey the smart-arsed George Michael look-alike. It was a three-pronged attack as there were only three of us. One on the lmg, and two with slr's and smoke grenades, that's the light machine gun and the good old L1a1 self-loading rifle. We were to pick them up from the stores Sergeant who was in long wheel base land rover at the grid reference below,
 "Taff; here sort that grid me old china, Jock and me will sort out who's on the lmg and who's throwing smoke at the enemy etc etc etc".

 "Shall I do all the map reading then lads?" complained Taff,

 "Well you have come up trumps twice already haven't you, and you know where all the sheep are! "
    "Bog off Weazel"
 "Oh come on Taff mate "

I pinched his ear and almost pulled it off messing about, he wasn't impressed.

"Right are you on the lmg Jock"

" Looks like it dunnit, come on let's tidy up this fire and mess and get going we need to meet   Sergeant Alfreton to get the gats (Rifles) and prep this ambush".

One piece of equipment in the package was a pair of binoculars which none of the other groups had which was handy because that meant that we could see them coming from a long distance and figure out which route they would take and scrim up accordingly then take positions and wait. So we were continually searching for other groups and anything else we could see,

"There's the Land Rover over there look"

"Well spotted Jock let's make our way over there then" Jock replied with the slightest hint of sarcasm,

"Ken that's a good idea".

"Are you ever going to tell me who this bloke Ken is any time this year Jock"

"Well I could do; but I'd have to kill you! Nah, it would mean that I would have to explain half the Scottish language to you which is far too intelligent for a wee Sassenach like yourself "

"Bloody Sassenach ha ha "

A roar of laughter brought on more hysterics and piss take remarks on Wales, Scotland and well, insignificant Chorley that it was.

"Good afternoon Sergeant Alfreton"

Corporal Camilari was also there to whom we nodded as a greeting,

"You missed a cracking chicken and carrot butty Corporal",

"Butty; where, prey where did you get the bread from to make a butty Winnels?"

"Taff made it Corporal"

"I see, so you have a portable oven, flour and yeast in that bergen have you, you 'orrible little Welshman. Sergeant have you given chitty's for any portable oven's recently, no thought not, nor have you signed out any flour and yeast, certainly not to these reprobates, what shall we do with em sergeant send em up the hill?"

This was generally the punishment for contraband bread that wasn't issued in the rations,

"Corporal I think it was actually chicken, leek and carrot stew that we had, can't remember any bread come to think of it and definitely no mushrooms. Are there some weapons here for us?"

Desperately trying to change the subject.

"Right, you have one lmg with blank firing attachment, two slr's also with blank firing attachments, plus four smoke grenades for the use of creating smoke. Sign there, put your name or your mark on the dotted line, take your chitty and of you go to play soldiers" Sergeant Alfreton said.

The bfa's were attached to the end of the rifles and allowed us to fire the weapon using blank rounds with safety, but they were painted bright yellow and could be seen for miles. Unfortunately the element of surprise would be rebuffed unless the enemy were completely blind or were members of parliament, blind and dumb!

We decided to scrim the bfa's with local foliage just to make us feel better and hopefully show initiative.

The intended ambush point as per the map was approximately one mile away on the path next to the river so we sat down and took a moment to assess the ground in front. Following behind approximately two hundred meters was corporal Camilari who I presume was observing, but not interfering yet with our preparation and planning of the hit. I asked Jock for the binocs and had a quick shifty around the fields and surrounding woods for any of the other groups, but could not see any sign. We decided between us that I should go up to the brow of the nearest hill with the binocs and view the whole area.

I don't know why, but the lyrics from T'pau's China in your hand came in to my head. Something about to push too far your dreams, where on earth that came from I'll never know, but it distracted me and I ended up walking into a bog which came almost up my knees and stunk like a pig sty.

I was slipping and sliding about and ended up losing my balance and fell into the bog backwards and slightly sideways, just managing to keep my gat (rifle) above everything so it kept clean, unfortunately the binocs didn't. They ended up absolutely covered in cack, all but the strap. I stood up and held the important piece of equipment I had been given to spot the enemy and watched the black treacle like mange drip off.

What I didn't even look at and wasn't even concerned about, was the state of my dpm smock and pants, I just said to myself the most descriptive word I could think, "SHIT"!

I manoeuvred my way through the rest of the bog aiming towards the foot of the hill, my gat strap was now over my shoulders holding the rifle to the right of my stomach which was the cleanest area of clothing I had. The binocs were being cleaned of a fashion with some doc leaves I had picked up a few steps ago. What I would give to be in the Game Bird pub in Euxton, near my home town. The place to be if you were anyone, well at least on a Thursday or a Sunday night anyway.

At the top of the hill I crouched behind a three-foot stone wall with a football sized hole. The view was pretty good as I scoped the landscape, searching for anything that was moving. Apart from livestock, there was nothing for about five minutes. I glanced back at Jock and Taff's position and could just about see them still laughing at my bog trip, I don't believe they saw me fall into that pile of crap, typical! I was about to stand up and water the grass, when something in the distance caught my eye. Following a line of trees were four bright yellow objects about two or three feet off the ground. They looked to be about a mile or so away. I could just about make out why I thought they were being carried in mid-air, it was one of the other groups flashing their bfa's about. I used my photographic memory and made a mental note of their position and estimated their time of arrival at the ambush point and made my way back to Taff and Jock avoiding the bog this time.

"Oh you managed to get back then without falling over did you" said Taff,

"What's that smell? No way is it you? What did you fall in cow pat or summat did you? You smelly bastard"

"Shut up a minute one of the other groups are coming and they aren't too far away we need to get prepped "! Taff are you taking the lmg (light machine gun)or what" ?

"Oh, shall I take the lmg shall I" Yeah I'll take the lmg then".

We made our way to the ambush point keeping in line with the trees and picking up local foliage as we went along and sticking it anywhere we could find a place. We definitely did not want them to see us. Even if the ambush failed, at least we would pass the camouflage and concealment part of the exercise. We must have looked like three long haired yetis. About one hundred yards from the point, we knelt down and discussed our options.

"Jock do you think it's worth doing this at a point which is not the recommended point, what I mean is, they might be expecting us to attack here, so should we not move the point to another location instead?"

I said,

"Yeah that's not a bad idea why didn't I think of that, what do you reckon Taff?

Taff replied with his annoying repetitiveness.

"Yes, I think we should attack from a different position as they will be expecting us to attack from the original one"

I looked at Jock in amazement. How would we manage for humour without this Welshman?

"You have shrewd warrior tactics Taff you should become a General very quickly after basic training"

"Right Taff, you take the lmg up to your position. Up to the right of the path near that mound of old house ruin there in a flank position. Jock and I will sit tight more or less there amongst the two trees with a gate in the middle. Wait for our signal then give short bursts until they give up, we'll throw a smoke grenade up and capture the gits before they can decide to escape"!

By this time Corporal Camilari had moved from his watching position and was almost spitting distance from us. In a low tone voice, he said

"What are you doing here? You are supposed to be five hundred metres down the road"

"Well corporal, it's a long story but Taff said it was a good idea and we believed him"

"Where is the daft Welsh twat"?

"He's took position in the old house ruin over there Corporal",

"Soddin 'ell, well he may as well stay there then. Right you two, bury yourself in those trees over there, the others are on their way just around the corner. Give me one of those smoke grenades just in case"

There was only one way they could come in down the path, so there should be no mistake in positions, I thought, as Jock and I sat behind the two trees trying to spot Taff so that we could give him a signal to fire.

We could hear them now, talking amongst themselves, the group of unsuspecting squaddies on exercise. I could just about hear mention of bed blocks and broomsticks and all other ablution duties that come with this job. It must end soon there can't be many days left of this bullshit. It would appear that they didn't like it here.

I nodded to Jock and with a big throw like a discus, swung the smoke grenade through the air. It landed just beyond the third man. Taff opened fire almost immediately, not even giving the smoke enough time to cover their view. Almost perfectly timed bursts of two to three seconds, which would have kept a battalion of enemies heads down had they been live rounds. Jock and I joined the affray and let out a full magazine each just for good measure.   The second smoke grenade was thrown by

Jock, the signal to charge and gain captives. All four of them seemed to give up fairly easily and without resistance as they didn't know what all the noise was about.

Corporal Camilari appeared from nowhere and shouted.
"STOP! You lot are dead. Make your way up that hill in quick time. I want you back here for a debrief in no less than twenty minutes"

The hill was about 3 miles round trip. They didn't have a chance of making it in twenty minutes. It was generally known that they would go up again until they were just about ready to drop. At least it wasn't raining now; you had to think positive in this game to get you through and of course the thought of seeing your girl again, if you had one. If you hadn't, then the thought of getting one helped.

"Private Mernie, get your bivvi pan out and make yourself and your mate wippleswip a brew. I'll go and get Taff"

Taff was slowly walking down from his position with an isosceles triangular shaped expression on his face. Chuffed as a parrot he was all that excitement, the noise, the smoke. Makes a man want to; Well, smile, like he's done a sort of good job.

Taff never used the word job, it wasn't part of his vocabulary. He openly admitted to detesting the word, couldn't say it without being sick, he said. He would use other words like task, mission or work or other descriptions.

"What do you reckon Taff Successful mission or what!"

"Yes successful mission don't you know boyo, thoroughly enjoyable isnit"

Spoken with a proper welsh accent,
 "Here have a cup of tea you daft welsh bugger"
 I passed him the cup which was the top part of the G10 issue water bottle, and Taff slowly lifted it as though it was a gold trophy with which he caressed and held up in jubilation,
"Cheers"

Corporal Camilari was waiting for the runners to come back from the trip round the top of the hill and I presume see us all back to the next RV point. He barked at us, I think because we were all sat down laughing about our conquest.
 "Right you 'orrible lot, get your act together sort out your shit and get a move on to the next RV. What do you think it is Muldoon's picnic?" We didn't wait around to see what happened to the group we ambushed. We picked up our shit and marched off. The next RV was a bridge too far. It was miles away from anywhere.

At the bridge we met Sergeant Hunter, who I think must have had a few swigs of his hip flask while waiting for us as he sounded like a Dalek when he said,

"The next stage of this exercise is camouflage and concealment and is designed to teach you how to blend in with the local environment. As you are already scrimmed up, all you have to do is crawl through that field and shoot that target on the brow without being seen by Corporal Thompson who is watching with binoculars to your left flank. Make sure you do a good job, help each other out, dress each other up, paint your war faces. Here are your live rounds, get them loaded into these

Slr's, pass those bfa slr's over here and get on your way, come on, sort it out"

The tall grass was still wet from a previous rainfall and stuck to our clothes, which made crawling a little bit more uncomfortable than normal. It was very difficult keeping low and looking where we were going, especially with a rifle to carry and keep off the wet ground. Every inch crawled seemed to take forever and there was at least a football field of distance to go. This has got to be the most nerve-racking training game since I last played monopoly.

Our arms were folded in front of us and in a criss cross movement in conjunction with our legs gripping the ground, pushed us forward. Rifles were placed on top of our arms. It seemed to work, albeit very slow, but we were not seen amongst the lengths of grass and reeds which had odd heights of between six inches and three foot. There were small mounds of earth left by rabbits or moles burrowing out their nests, and dried cow pat from previous cattle grazing.

My neck was beginning to ache now from looking forward and trying to see where the spotter was, but to no avail, as long as he didn't see us that is all that mattered. I kept on crawling forward over cow pat, mud, and puddles of water which began to stink. We were definitely blending in. We were told by Sergeant Hunter that if we were seen there would first be a whistle blown then someone would run to the spot where the spotter thought we were. We hadn't heard a whistle yet.

Taff was approximately seven feet away and Jock about the same. Jock looked at me and gave the sign which was a round circle and five fingers; he must be able to see the target and was saying that it was fifty foot away. I looked at Taff to make sure he acknowledged the signal. We all brought our weapons forward into an aiming position and prepared to fire whilst edging very slowly forward into direct sight of the target. Safety catches off, Bang Bang Bang Bang Bang Bang!! Apparently, there were twenty-two shots fired at the cardboard cut-out before we heard the whistle blow. I could see Sergeant Hunter running towards us from the rear, so we stood up and looked at the obliterated target.

"Do you think we were on target then Taff?

"We certainly got that boyo didn't we"

Jock was looking at Sergeant Hunters war face before he reached our position,

"What the bloody ell do think you are playing at you dickheads. Just look at the state of my pussers target you trio of boneheaded twats! I wanted that target to last till the end of the exercise, Bloody Ell"! He turned away in disgust and dismay, thought about punishment and looked at us and pointed up the hill.

"You've got twenty-five minutes".

We could still here him cursing us and chunnering to himself like an old woman as we made our way up the hill.

"Bunch of wankers, poxy bloody pig-headed trigger-happy twats"

What had we done wrong, I'm sure he said try and shoot the target when we get close? "Come on let's get this over with"

I tried to install a bit of enthusiasm to the other two with a little bit of success as we set off at a cracking pace. Taff looked around and could see Sergeant Hunter moaning to Corporal Thomson. Thomson was just nodding in agreement and approval or disapproval not sure which one but sure as hell we would find out when we got back. Sergeant Hunter was waiting for us at the end of the hill top trip,

"I suppose you think you are smart, do you? breaking the battalion record for that hill. I also suppose you think you are proper soldiers being the only ones that didn't get noticed by Corporal Thomson scrimmed up in the field, well you are not! Get down, give me twenty and then you can carry this jerry can full of water to your next RV."

Not knowing what we did wrong we picked up the can and made for the next rv. The jerry can was of course a five gallon one but weighed about seven tons or at least it seemed so.

"Taff here give us that can, Jock and I will carry that while you sort out where we are going"

"Right you are, here, I'll pass you the can for a minute while I sort out where we are going"

Taff's repetitiveness would be so annoying if you didn't know him, it was as though he was just making sure everybody knew that it was his idea in the first place. I looked at Jock with a slight head shake and tut. He agreed that we were associated with a very intelligent astronaut brain professor person, what a shame we left him at home!

"Right then, let's see now, where is that tree on this map? Oh yes, there Is the, no wait, it must be there above the contour here......right, up there by the fence is a style over the fence"

"That must be a public footpath Taff"

"Yes well we go over there and then follow the path for two miles and then take a right at the broken fence and then there is a wood which we have to..."

I stopped him there, bored already,

"Ok Taff we'll follow you"

By the time we had reached the style, Jock and I had a little sweat about us. The weight of the water filled jerry can was pushing down on my right shoulder and Jock's left shoulder. We were walking behind the other which was almost awkward, we tried not to trip over each other's feet and then manhandled the can over the style well ok we threw it over the fence, then trampled over the style with gat's in hand skeleton webbing around our waist and looked at Taff for direction, Jock preceded to place his rifle through the jerry can handle as a makeshift carrying cradle which I picked up one side at the same time as he picked up the other and nodded to him in approval. We had our reconnaissance platoon heads on and were scouring all around the area for other groups, the front man looked ahead and in a 180 degrees arc left and right and the person behind viewed right in a 180 degrees arc overlapping the front man's forward arc slightly and to the right and behind, and the next man in line viewed left in a 180 degrees arc covering any missing landscape not covered by anybody else, this of course worked better with more than three as at least one would be map reading, but we had Taff our secret welsh weapon, who after looking at a map once could get from Swansea to Mold in the shortest time possible without any fuss.

All one had to do was put up with his continual inane gibberish and his involuntary displays of macho acting skills which involved the Bruce lee karate stance and a Shakespearean type verbal descriptive combination of different languages rolled into one sentence meaning the same thing. No problem we thought. At least we will beat the others.

"Are we there yet"? I asked Taff

"Don't be impatient boyo, not far now"

I think he was a bit miffed because he hadn't seen any sheep for a while and was feeling a bit homesick or summat.
All of a sudden Taff swept his arm from his waist in a roundhouse movement with open hand up to head height
 "Il le ya le rv, the meeting point"

Jock looked at me and said to Taff,
 "Ken there's no one there"
  "Well that's it don't you know" Taff argued.

We placed our kit and jerry can on the floor at the rv and had a good stretch and muscle moan and cursed the jerry can for being so heavy, and looked around, to the front and to the right were flat fields and clear vision, but to the left was a big hill with trees at the bottom and some flower patches were scattered about here and there. The hill had a very steep gradient about sixty percent which was covered with long grass. I could see us running up there as punishment for being in the wrong place.
Jock and me were looking at each other wondering who was going to ask Taff if he was sure this is the right place, then we were disturbed by a noise coming from on top of the hill, we all looked up and could see in the distance a land rover being driven on the ridge on top of the hill, it pulled up slowly and stopped and we could see the

passenger pointing down the hill at his driver as though he was saying to him quickest route to that location. Then the gearbox crunched into four-wheel drive and a quick rev of the 2.2 petrol engine and a 90 degrees left turn and the vehicle made a high-pitched transmission whine as it came down the hill in high ratio mode to get minimum torque at the wheels and maximum safety

About half way down the hill we could now make out the passenger wore a light brown shirt with the collar in a Shaking Stevens type fashion.

"Bloody ell it's Captain Manwearing and his sidekick Pike" I said to the others.

They of course knew I was referring to Captain Macintosh and his driver Ht, short for High Tower because he was in fact about nine feet tall and had to bow his head whilst driving and also had two metal teeth and a bent nose to add to his oddness, what a matching pair!

The Land Rover's descent finished in classic four-wheel drive position, one front wheel placed inadvertently on a mound of earth lifting the vehicle up about two feet in the air on one corner, the obtuse angle forced the door to swing open more rapidly than normal, out came the Captain

"What's your name Private"

"Private Mernie Sir"

"Right private Mernie Tell me how the hell have you got to this location so quickly, I've just spoken to Sergeant Hunter at your last location on the walkie talkie's and you should not be here for about another hour, who has picked you up and given you a lift ?"

By this time the captain has turned around and slammed the land rover door shut making high tower's head roll side to side with the vibration which was well amusing to say the least as it was already in forward march position and mouth grinning with the delight of picking up three potential pvr's and shoving them in the back of the land rover.

"Well Private Mernie what have you got to say for yourself, and you two get down and give me 50"

I looked at Taff and whispered that's what we get for laughing at Herman Munster behind the wheel.

"Well Sir we just followed the grids on the map Sir"

"Bollocks I want to know how you got here so quick Man, who did the map reading?"

I had managed twenty-seven press ups and was now struggling to lift up from the floor without pulling a strain face and keep my breath but somehow managed to look up and squeeze out the words,

"Me sir I did the map reading sir"

"Right up you get man and you fella"

Taff jumped up in quick time, grateful for not having to do any more press ups and looked at me with puzzlement, I could tell he was wondering why I admitted to the map reading...Captain Mackintosh looked at Taff who was sweating profusely now,

"You will do the map reading from now on and we will be watching you, right that jerry can needs to be left here my land rover has a water leak but first fill your water bottles up. Get that bonnet up high tower"

The captain managed to bark his last order out of a partially opened mouth which was pointed in Ht's direction, can't let the golf ball fall out now can we? We took a drink from our newly filled olive green pusser's flask and were given our new grids by High Tower who was ever so disappointed that he didn't get any more pvr's Ht walked off towards the land rover after quietly warning us of enemy forces in or around the aqueduct which was of course on our route.

"Right Taff what's the plan Mr map reader? Considering the potential ambush at the aqueduct?"

"let me have a look see I'll not be a minute just need to err, mm, err just a minute err right that's that thing there and we go to here then half mile up there, mag to grid get rid an all that."

Jock and I looked in amazement at the professor at work and listened to him talking to himself and thought if and when we had kids we must send them to the same school as Taff, we would be chuffed if they came out with only half the brains as this man has. Taff led us away and informed us that he would take us an indirect route to the aqueduct so we could recce the situation and appraise it accordingly. All of a sudden Jock looked at me and said

"Ken you still stink of cow shit ya smelly bassa "

"Well unfortunately I've not had time for a shower since the crawling about in the bog at that target practice, after this is over I'll make sure I jump in the nearest bath just for you Jock"

Taff led us up this hill and stopped us to say when we get to the top we should see the battle area ahead, so we walked ahead carefully so as not to be seen by anybody, I looked down at a big puddle which seemed to be about three inches deep, which as it happens was the exact depth required for me to dip the cow pat covered binoculars I had been hiding from the Rank and Rodney's at each Rv, now would be a good time to get them out and hope they would survive the bath they were about to get,

 "Hey, you two, hang about let's see if I can clean these a min"

I dragged the Bergen off my back and dug to the bottom and pulled out a dried-up pile of crap stuck to a rectangular shaped moulded plastic mess!

"Bloody ell Weal's, what the Fick is that"?

"That my old china is, one G10 issue pussers bino's for the use of seeing enemy with innit"

"Looks more like a pile of dried up cow pat"

Taff said

"And it's Welsh Black cow pat as well"

"Well you don't need to remind us that you are the authority on dried up cow pat Taff"

"I'm telling you boyo that's Celtic ass shit that is"

After several moments of laughter Jock replied to the man of knowledge,

"Ken you're a Celtic ass man"

I tried to clean and scrape the crap of the bino's, so they were at least useable, I even had to borrow the mini pliers from Jock's Swiss army knife to pull away the awkward bit of shit from one of the eyepiece lenses before giving them to Taff to look through

"Oh I see "

Taff said with enlightenment

"You want me to?"

"Yes"

We both interrupted and nodded at each other in mutual approval.   Both Jock and Taff found this soldiering lark natural, they were both very fit, clever, and had plenty of common sense, and a taste for humour which sometimes made me feel a bit inferior, I on the other hand had to work at it a bit more, but still enjoyed it never the less.

We approached the brow of the hill on all fours and peered over the top, we were determined to get two rings of cow pat, sorry Celtic cow pat on Taff's eye sockets, where he had put the bino's to his head to see but he was being very careful not touch anything with the smelly articles.

"What can you see Taff"

"I can see two of my mates making a brew"!

"Eh, where? oh right, cheeky arse right Jock get mess tins out man and bivvy pack we'll have a brew, have you any rat pack chocolate left"?

"Nah scoffed it didn't I, didn't think anybody else liked that but me",

"Doh, I was just looking forward to something sweet, never mind, it will have to be a rat pack garibaldi instead then, tea and biscuits just like home !! "

Taff spent a good five minutes looking through the bino's muttering to himself and trying to weigh up what he saw and how to describe it to us,

"Here boys have a look,"

"It's ok you can tell us what you saw, we believe you",

"Well it's like this see, there is a cabin with no windows to the left of the grounds with two guards outside walking around outside it and a trailer with a canopy over it near the back door, then there is a hill blocking the cabin from view of the wood and its surroundings, then there is an aqueduct to the right, now then there are two different sections of men at each end of the aqua duct both sat down behind cover looking very shifty like, there is a path or small road running through the third arch at the north of the aqueduct and I can also see a Bedford 4 tonner and a land rover parked approximately five hundred metres to the west of the path on the south side of the aqueduct".

"Bloody ell Taff are you sure you haven't missed anything out?" "

Oh yes err Corporals Camilari and Thomson, Sergeant Hunter and Captain Macintosh are on the aqueduct watching everything, the Captain has an antenna growing out of his ear",

What the ell is he doing on his walkie talky this time, calling in air support?

We were guessing that the two sections of men at either side of the aqueduct were there to ambush us and possibly had already done so to the other groups of recruits, could have even took prisoners and maybe they were in the cabin under guard. We also presumed that the vehicles were there to pick us up as the exercise was almost finished, so we all briefed ourselves and made a drawing in the soil by our feet of our battle plan.

"Jock have you got any ammo or smoke grenades left"?

"No, used em all"

I then looked at Taff and he said the same,

"Ok, what do you reckon to raiding the cabin and the trailer to see if we can't find summat to fight the enemy with"?

Taff replied with

"Yes, it's supposed to be off limits according to the map but let's raid the cabin to see what that's got"

We spent a good fifteen minutes scouring the local ground for foliage, fallen leaves, twigs, twine anything that made us look like we blended in Chameleon style, we spent another fifteen minutes dressing ourselves with the scrim and we checked each other out and made sure our war paint matched the scrim. Happy with our camouflage we set off towards the cabin with the intent of acquiring some sort of Ambush aid.

It took us nearly an hour and a half to track down to the cabin, although to just get up and walk it would have taken fifteen minutes, great care was taken to not be seen by the guards, slow crawling was the order of the day, one behind each other, each forward arm stroke was a form of art, before the hand touched the floor it had to scrape sideways any loose ground so as not to snap any small twigs which could be heard from a fair distance in front, and would alert the guards, similar movements were made with our legs which exhausted us but was necessary, we could not be seen! Total silence throughout the crawl.

The cabin was now in sight and the two guards, we could also see the door had no padlock on it but an old style barn door shutting mechanism, which was basically a piece of four by one inches plank of wood rested over two u-brackets, one either side of the door, so it looked like getting in was as easy as lifting the piece of wood., we were that close we could hear laughter from inside the cabin which only confirmed our earlier suspicions.

Taff and Jock gave me the military sign language saying that they would take on the guards and as soon as they were down I had to open the cabin door and see who was inside. They creeped towards the guards and waited till they had their backs to them and then they pounced, Jock was almost on all fours when he dived towards the guard on the right kicking his legs from under him, this brought him down straight away, his body buckled and landed with a thud on the floor, he then rolled over on top of him and held him in a neck lock judo type hold, he was going nowhere. Taff meanwhile was struggling to get his man under control, he had him in an arm lock but the other arm was punching him repetitively in the arm making his muscle dead, I ran towards him and pushed the guard to the floor who then said

"Alright alright you got us"

"Yep we definitely got You, get up Taff before you start going to sleep"! It was now the guards turn to swap places with the captives, I opened the door and told everyone to get out, there was a resounding cheer,

"Yeah about time weasel"

"Ay up Taff",

scouse Roberts came out along with scouse Moran and Scouse Wilson, then came Dan the man Dooley from Doncaster, and Alan Braithwaite from Shipley and last but not least Andy White (Chalky) he was from somewhere unpronounceable near Bristol,

"How long have you lot been in there then",

"Those three about an hour, and the rest of us about three hours"

"Bloody ell, I bet you were bored shitless weren't you"?

"It wasn't too bad, there is a window round the back and we could see what is going on"

"Excellent, so what is going on then"?

Chalky went on for about half an hour about how they were captured by the recruits who were three weeks training ahead of us, and put in the cabin to await further orders, meanwhile, Taff and Jock were both putting the two guards in the cabin making sure they had brew making facilities and rat packs and no hard feelings, they were actually sick notes from an earlier platoon on light duties to heel their injuries.

"So Chalky are there just the two attack squads to look out for"?

"Nah, there are four in total, the two you can see on either side of the aqueduct are a decoy but may still be deployed for assistance, soon after we were captured and marched here, the four groups split up and I'm just not sure where the other two are".

"Ok nice one, that's well useful information, and do the instructors know that you have been captured"?

"Oh Yeah definitely"

"Here Taff, Jock, we'll have to do some master plan here there's another two squads of Attack platoon here knocking about somewhere"

"Yeah we know where an all" Jock said

"The guards told us that there is a tent to the west of the four tonner behind a small wood out of sight, and they told us that the trailer there (He pointed to the trailer behind him) is full of climbing equipment, flares, a few gats with bfa's and blank rounds.

"Oh and they gave me this,"

Taff produced a walkie talkie which although had a broken mike would be extremely useful to listen to what is going on,

"Wicked" I said

"Taff what's the geography lesson to be"

"Well we are supposed to be bimbling down the path which takes us through the third arch of the aqueduct, but as that path is now the ambush path, that route is out of the question, just give me a minute"

While Taff was doing the route, Jock and me were asking if the others who we rescued would pretend to be us and walk into the trap on the third arch path, well at least three of them anyway, the three scousers agreed to do it, they were thick as thieves and didn't mind staying together even if it was to get ambushed, they also knew that as soon as the attack squadron realised that they had ambushed these three before, they would know that the joke was on them.

"Right scouse what we want you to do is to make a bit of an effort to not get seen easily, so as to make them think you are us and lull them into a false sense of security, then hopefully they might only get to see your faces when you are twenty feet away, giving us a chance to do some no good elsewhere, have you done Taff?

"Err yes I've done, I think so yes, err just a minute, just putting final touches to Yep finished".

" So we are going around the aqueduct and to the left then will end up following the small wood to which the small tent is, Innit" Now the grid given is by my reckoning exactly where the vehicles are parked, so tent first, vehicles second"   "Ok let's get cracking"

 I told the dodgy scousers to give us half an hour before setting off, and said to the others to hang around here for a bit but try and keep out of sight so we might be able to complete the course without getting caught, not like everybody else!

We had been walking about fifteen minutes when I saw some cows being led into a field and down a line of trees, by a farmer and two dogs,   and the line of trees seemed to go to the left of the aqueduct away from all other groups of people.

 "Here Taff, are those cows going the same way as we need to go can we use them as cover"

 "Yes we can use those cows as cover if we hurry up, come on then"

 We had to give it some to get on the other side of the cattle as they were about five hundred meters away, and we gave the farmer the shock of his life, he thought the cows had decided they weren't happy with four legs and decided to run with two instead and had grown instant

[45]

green and brown hair implants. He relaxed a bit realising what we were doing, as we were twenty feet apart and doing the job of two sheepdogs and staying out of sight of anybody with bino's , we crouched down so our heads were just below the height of the cows and managed to cover two fields worth of distance under natural cover, brilliant ! We broke off from the cattle, and Taff looked back as he was struggling to define the origin or ilk of the beasts.

"Hmmm, not sure about those I think they are Dexter's, yep dirty black sods Dexter's don't you know"
"What are you are going on about Taff, Jock tell him to stop wittering!"
"Taff stop wittering, which way next"

Taff still had the LMG which was heavier than our SLR's so Jock swapped and told me I was next.   We couldn't even see the Bedford four tonner now, we had done a left flank with the cows and ended up at the beginning of the small wood on the other side of the aqueduct, so we knew that if we could get through the wood the tent full of the enemy should be on the other side.

"Taff are we taking a compass reading or what"?
   "Right boys hold it there we'll take a compass reading before we get in the thick of it"
Taff said with his "I've just had a brainwave voice".

"As long as we don't go off course the tent and vehicles should be about one mile north north east of our location"
"Quiet a min I can hear someone on this walkie talkie thing" Sergeant Hunter was moaning to the two Corporals that he couldn't see us anywhere, and that

made me think that the three stooges I mean scousers should be setting off by now on their decoy patrol.

We set off through the woods as fast as we could following Taff's compass reading regularly checking it as it is very easy to go off course particularly in forest terrain, Taff slowed up momentarily just to stretch out his heel, apparently his foot was stuck in a rabbit hole and he hobbled for a few feet to walk it out, then back to normal jogging pace, we picked up a small path which led over a narrow river just about enough water in it for trout, shame we didn't have time for fishing. We continued on and on until approaching an electric barbed wire fence, Taff checked the map and compass and reassured us that the way we need to go is straight ahead over the fence and to the right and pick up the path again.

"How many volts in this fence Taff"?

"They generally have about 5000 volts running through but it's only a pulse"

"Oh that's alright then!"

Jock was looking down the line of the fence for some sort of connector or transformer or something to unplug,

"Here lads get over this"

I stretched down and grabbed hold of the bottom of one of the fence spindles and lifted it then pushed the wood forward, fortunately the wire was loose enough to allow the fence to bend over enough for the boys to dive over and hold at the top for me to do the same.

The fence was the only obstacle in our path and was at the top of a hill so the route forward was taken fairly quickly as we were running downhill and making good time. Jock was in front about ten foot but slowed down and turned towards us and said

"Listen, Captain Macintosh has seen the scousers and deployed the first attack squad"

"Shit, that gives us about fifteen minutes to get to the tent before they get deployed"
"Come on then"
We ran like the clappers for about ten minutes and managed to get to a point where we could see the four tonner, we then looked left but could not yet see the tent, we were getting close, so we decided to slow down to create less noise and keep our eyes peeled.

"Taff the tent should be to the left shouldn't it" I said in a low voice.

Jock was still up front and turned around and gave us the, "be quiet" signal and the sign to the ears to listen.

"Listen to that can you hear them laughing, they are up there I can hear at least three of em and one of them has just been for a piss, right get into crawl order again and get ready with the last smoke grenade"!

Crawling into position wasn't difficult this time because they were making that much noise they wouldn't have heard us anyway. We managed to get into a semi-circle on the outside of the tent entrance and threw in the smoke grenade, all we could hear was a load of coughing and swearing then five men came running out,

"You bastards, Bloody Ell just a come out with your hands up would have done"!
Still loads of coughing and swearing. We all stood up and pointed our weapons and Taff shouted
"Hande Hoch"
Then started laughing, with which the now prisoners put their hands up still coughing and cursing, so we

marched them off` to the Bedford four tonner which was about thirty foot away and shoved them in the back and strapped them in with the tarpaulin over the back.

Just then Jock heard a crackle from the radio then the croaky voice of Sergeant Hunter whose baseline almost shattered the speaker with its vibration.

"Attack squad listen in, enemy approaching the third arch ambush and apprehend immediately, over"

We heard this command in stereo as we borrowed the radio off the squad we had just put in the truck so it was a double decibel order.

"Message received and understood out"

By this time Taff was looking through the binoculars at Captain Macintosh and the nco's walking off the top of the Aqueduct and down an embankment to the ground level, I would suspect to give the scousers a bollocking thinking they were us.

"Taff lets creep up and follow behind to listen to what goes on with the scousers"

"Shall we go and see what happens with the scousers boys"

Taff replied with yet again the annoying repetitiveness which everybody knew was his personality shining through.

Bang bang bang bang bang! There was loads of shouting, we could here and just about see the ambush, good old scousers we thought.

"Bloody ell it's you lot again, you are supposed to be in the cabin you wankers, who let you out"?

"Err well it's like this mate, err there were these three blokes right and they said they would give us a pack of ciggies if we walked down this path here like, you know" Scouse Moran said in a very broad Liverpudlian accent

"What a load of bullshit, what three blokes"?

"Err where did them three blokes go la"?

"Dunno la"

The scousers kept looking at each other for about what seemed like five minutes with amnesiac faces, questioning themselves, were there actually three or two can't remember might have only been one. One of the attack squad looked around to see if Captain Macintosh was anywhere, and there he was walking towards the commotion and disturbance and the aftermath of what was supposed to be the last ambush. Sergeant Hunter, Corporals Thomson and Camilari in tow. The Captain looked at Scouse Moran and barked

"Name"?

"Moran sir"

"Well Moron where the Hell are Mernie, Wealan and that Welshman whatever his name is"

"Err, not sure they were up at the cabin haven't seen them since"!

"Bloody ell! Sergeant Hunter can you possibly deal with this utter cock up I'm going to be late for my barbers appointment, and when you find the three musketeers send them to my office at 20.42hrs if you don't mind"

"Right you are sir"

"Where is high tower"?

"Looks like he's watering that tree over there sir"

"Come on High Tower put it away and get me to my bonnet cut"

Captain Macintosh was driven away at high speed to the local beauticians which doubled up as a sunbed parlour and haircropshop with which he frequented.

"What do you reckon Taff should we just jump up and at em or shall we do a sneaky beaky on em"?

 Jock Mernie interrupted and suggested that we just sit in the middle of the path and wait for them to turn around, and realise that we had been there all the time just hidden in the undergrowth. So we got up from our lying down positions and bimbled over to the middle of the path.

"You three get up of your arse's and get here you miscreants, how the hell have you not been seen or ambushed , where the hell have you been, who told you to let these three scousers out of the cabin, I thought we'd got rid of their bullshit for a while, get up the hill you have twenty minutes"

 Sergeant Hunter was not impressed by our skill and expertise in the exercise or so it seemed. Off we went up the hill as if we weren't knackered enough, starving, and desperately in need of the five s's.   Sergeant Hunter led everyone else except for Corporal Camilari over to the Bedford and told them to get in, had another moan this time about the attack squad being put in the back of the duty transport,

 "Get out you lot and make your way to the cabin collect your mates on the way, and wait for your own bus"

By that he meant the other three attack squads who would be getting bored by now and wondering what the earlier gunfire was.

[51]

Corporal Camilari decided to give us a bit of his sarcastic enthusiasm by shouting out at us for the last five hundred metres of our punishment.

"keep running, keep running, keep running, keep running, keep running, Keep running"!

We did and we arrived in record time again.

"What are you sweating for Taff anybody would think you had just been on a run or summat, no room in this section for sweaty boys , don't want the whiff of your b.o putting us all off now do we, and you Wippleswip what's wrong with you man? Stand up, you are in bits, pull yourself together you bone headed skeleton, get a grip"! Sort your act out before I decide to pvr you, bloody Scottish, welsh and then there is you Wealywoo pull your finger out Man"

I think he was trying to demoralise us in his own special way, putting us to the test, attacking our morale and personality to see if we would break, but he knew we wouldn't

"Alright get yourself over there near that truck, men"

Another land rover had arrived and had been left next to the Bedford four tonner, which was now setting off.

Corporal Camilari jogged with us to the rover and told us to get in. We set off Corporal in the driving seat Taff` in the front passenger seat and followed the Bedford.

"Not many big tests to do now lads, just about four then you are through to the last week or so"

"What might those tests be Corporal"?

I asked with anticipation and dread

"Well that would be telling wouldn't it, all exciting stuff but it does include a party at the local wrac college"

W.r.a.c college" Taff puzzled   "Yeah something you screw against a wall" Jock replied

"Oh that will be good I like DIY"

Me Jock and Corporal Camilari turned towards each other and burst into laughter,

"What you laughing at boyo"?

"Never mind"

About two miles down the road Corporal Camilari approached a junction, stopped, and asked Taff if the road was clear.

"Is it clear Taff"?

"Yes,   there is a car coming !"

"Shit, Bloody ell Taff ,   I'm half way across the road now, maybe next time you are asked a question like "is it clear" would it be possible for you to not leave a huge gap in the word yes and, there is a car coming"?

Corporal Camilari complained.

In-between laughing Jock spoke

"Ken he's Welsh, you're better off asking that steering wheel at least you will get a roundabout answer"

We arrived back at base and were told to hand all gats in to Sergeant Alfreton in the armoury and then get into pt. kit, that being lightweights, boots and V-neck red t-shirt. More pt.   The whistle blew which meant get outside on parade ready for pt.   Sergeant Hunter croaked at us in dalek tone once more.

"Left turn, double march"

Twelve of us there was in the squad, and we wondered what sort of pt. this would be after all that stuff we had just done.   About half a mile away from the barracks, but still in the grounds was an assault course which we all looked at whilst still running and thought didn't look that exhausting and didn't have many large obstacles to get over, then we were halted and ordered to walk to the left and arrange ourselves into three ranks, and there they were lying on the ground almost hidden by the grass, six twelve foot logs with a diameter of about one foot maybe more, full of nobbles and notches from previous escapades, travels and adventures.

"What you see in front of you are six logs, as there are only twelve of you, only three will be used, so, three four man teams with one team leader, each team picks up the log and places it on the shoulders of three men, using the fourth team member as a reserve, the log and the team must get over all obstacles on the assault course, this is a practice for next week when you will be tested along with the other four tests which you must pass before being considered for parachute training." Sergeant Hunter barked.

I ended up in team one which was scouse Moran and souse Roberts, Andy White and myself, Taff and Jock were both in separate teams.

"Right team one and team three pick up your logs"
I asked the question to no one in particular,
"Which is the smallest, Sergeant."
"Shut it Wealtrim"

Bloody thing weighed a Ton, we looked at each other and thought this might be a bit awkward.

"Get up to the start line then, wait for it, wait for it"

Then the whistle blew.

The first three obstacles were fairly easy and were managed ok but then came the seven-foot wall. We could hear Corporal Thomson bellowing in our ears like a huge double bassoon

"Get that twig over that wall you wet lettuces, I didn't get where I am today by watching a bunch of women mincing about with a piece of wood and a few bricks, get a move on"

Scouse Moran gave me a leg up on to the wall, I jumped off his hand and made a stride over the top and pulled myself on top of the wall and sat down one leg dangling down each side of the wall hoping to help with the log when it was heaved up and over the red brick wall, which was slippy from previous rainfalls and lack of cleaning, it almost had mushrooms growing in the gaps where the mortar had eroded and discoloured, and when you have a log that possibly weighs about twenty stone it was a wee bit difficult.

Both scousers and chalky white were attempting to lift the log on top of the wall without much success, Chalky ended up getting them to put the log on his shoulder then his plan was to somehow walk it up the wall to me then help the other two at the bottom to lift it up.

"Here Scouse get that thing on my shoulder will you, and let's get moving we are behind already"
I could see a sharp and hurtful pain face in Chalky as the weight was plonked on his right shoulder, a speckle of blood draped across the gap between the log and his ear, one of the sharp nobbles had caught his lobe on the way down toward his shoulder, a small chunk of skin dangled down with more blood pouring out, Chalky cursed and

swore several times and pulled his right arm up and around the log to try and stop the log from falling off and to also hold his ear together, but the log was too thick and his arm didn't reach. The two scousers attempted to get under the log and lift it off chalkie's shoulder and on to the wall, the log was raised about a foot and I managed to get a hand under it and pull it towards me, it was then shoved up towards the top in an attempt to get it on top, about one third stayed in mid-air for a moment and then thumped on the top of the wall, all three of them went to the bottom of the log and again heaved it upwards letting out several war cries in the process, for a split second the log ended up midway on the wall with an equal distance dangling either side but rocking and rolling sideways and up and down like a see saw, I tried to grab the log and support it but the sheer weight of it did not allow it, scouse Moran thrust his arms up and around the log slipping in the mud at the base of the wall, his right arm caught the right side of the log as it was on its way to protect him from the acrobatic slip that threw him to the floor, the log spun again and toppled off the wall and slid down towards scouse Roberts who was unaware of it's descent, the log lodged itself in scouse Roberts's left side of his face forcing him down to the ground.

Blood splattered from his left nostril across his cheek and covered his neck. The log then bounced itself off a black, blue and red damaged face and onto both Scouse's' legs which made a resounding crack, and there was no scream of pain and no moaning.

Scouse Roberts was motionless and his bloody arms lay in an abstract position, his legs were trapped by the weight, his face had already ballooned into a red and blue mess, and he did not say a word he was out!

Corporal Camilari looked on in horror and blew his whistle for everyone to stop and ran over to help, I had jumped off the wall and with the help of Corporal Thompson, scouse Moran and chalky lifted the log off scouse Roberts frame and attempted to find a pulse and revive him, Sergeant Hunter had arrived on the scene and ordered Corporal Thompson to get the land rover and drive it as near as he could then get the stretcher out of the back as we would have to take him to hospital, we could now feel a pulse which was only slightly reassuring for a short moment, But no senses at all.

Scouse Moran was driven off with his mate in the back and we were told to make our way back to the barracks in double time, Log race cancelled.   We arrived at the barracks in shock mode, and needed something to lift the mood and the instructors knew it.

 "Right men listen in, right turn, double march, left right left right left right,"

  We set off in the direction of the football fields which were near the barber's portacabin   and were lined up in two ranks.

 "Right pair off with someone your own size, hurry up, come on hurry up, too slow get down give me twenty, right up you get, ok; Fireman's lift. look in bend down slightly back straight grab your partner's arm, any one, and place over your back following with his or hers chest and stomach,   your head should be under either of your partners armpits, then with whichever arm that is on the same side   as your partners frame, put through your partners legs and lift,   your partner can then grab your belt to stabilize himself and you can grab his other arm around your neck like so and then lift,   Right on you go"

"Get him up you Jessie; he only weighs about four stone"

There was lots of muscle moaning, swearing, cursing and at least two men dropped their partner before managing to lift them to the correct height stood up proper ready to go.

"Right you have one minute to get to the other side of the footy field, Go"

Corporal Camilari was good at explaining things. So we almost got it right. At least I did, well I must have because I was second to cross the line of the full-length football field.
The others were still half way and one was still in the goal line getting an ear bending from Sergeant Hunter.   We swapped partners and repeated the exercise again, it was very physically demanding so we all suffered some sort of pain, even Jock had a sweat on him. The recruits that had passed the line turned around and with their out of breath body and shouted enthusiasm to the stragglers and strugglers.

It was about two hours after the fireman's lift training that we had news on scouse. Corporal Camilari came in and found us cleaning gats, polishing boots, toilets, washing dpm kit, webbing and all other equipment including binoculars before they were handed back to the stores until next time.   He walked into our room and told us to relax as we stood up as we should when a member of staff walked in the room.

"Right men listen in, Scouse Roberts is now in a local civilian hospital in intensive care in a stable condition, so I'm sure he will be ok soon enough, now it was an accident so there will be no further repercussions, I'll let you know of any further developments. Now then anybody any problems with anything else, be sharp, tell me know then I can do something about it, you have one week before finals, then if you are one of the lucky ones you might get a crimson lid, then go on to jump out of a perfectly serviceable plane for some unknown reason".

"Corporal I've got a small problem"

"Evans unfortunately I can't do anything about the size of your male anatomy you will have to see the surgeon"

"No corporal I've got an even smaller problem"

"What's wrong with your brain then? Again you will have to see the surgeon I can't perform lobotomies"!

By this time everyone was in extreme laughter again, the humour around the boys was proper funny, I've never witnessed anything like it, laugh a minute over something ridiculous like a toothbrush left in a toilet or a broken boot lace on parade morning, the slightest mister meaner and a joke was created, a morale lifting statement, a mood boosting mix up of unknown vocabulary, anything to totally embarrass the unfortunate initial verbal administrator.

"What exactly is the problem Evans "?

"Erm, my girlfriends pregnant Corporal"

"You dozy twat, well you ain't gonna get no sympathy from me, how old are you? Well I can't do anything about that now can I, any more problems with anything else, no, good"

[59]

Corporal Camilari immediately turned and walked out of the room not giving anyone chance to answer. I think Evans was trying to tell the corporal that he was thinking of leaving to be with her but that idea was foreseen by our mentor and immediately rebuffed. Evans was from Anglesey in North Wales but for some reason seemed to think he was a scouser or he had a scouse accent leastways.

We continued to get on with polishing our boots and cleaning the bogs and de-dusting the floor and ironing lightweights for tomorrow's pt then, as it is the ten mile yomp with Bergen pack and gat, doh, sounds good, not.

"Here Taff, have you got my parade gloss pal"?

"One tin of parade gloss for the use of polishing one's boots as per requirement"

Passed to me with a fully outstretched right arm and torso thrust from the karate stance body of Taff the Welshman.

"Cheers Taff, by the way how much are you betting me that I'll win the shooting competition "?

"There's no point betting against someone who has never missed on the shooting range now is there"

"Well I do try my best and as there are only eleven left in our platoon there's not much competition is there?"

I had just finished polishing my boots and it was half past one in the morning and we all knew that we would be up at five thirty, but four hours sleep was about normal and had been throughout the duration of this training, I could only remember one lie in which was on a Sunday,   A few Sundays ago.!

It was four thirty when we were woken up with the two dustbin lids clattering together outside, has that Corporal no consideration for others!   Corporal Camilari came running up the stairs shouting the usual get up and go lingo.

"Come on you horrible bunch of lazy good for nothings, GET UP, outside in five mins pt kit, hurry up hurry up"

And off we were again, white t-shirt, lightweights and boots with elastics round the bottom. These elastics were the Armies' attempt at moving into the twenty first century and were an alternative and an improvement on the old puttee cloth which took about three hours to wrap around your ankle.   All eight of us were on BFT (Battle fitness test)   before breakfast, ah well at least it was only three miles in total.

"Right you orrible lot, BFT   one and a half miles as a squad in under fifteen minutes, then back in your own time as long as it's under fifteen minutes, you should all be doing this in under nine minutes, no excuses Wealan"
The first time he's called me by my proper name I don't believe it.
I came in behind Taff with a respectable time of eight minutes fifty seconds Jock Mernie was third at nine minutes two seconds, all the squad came in and we were dismissed for shower and breakfast another test passed with flying colours.

"Ah lovely my old favourite double poached eggs and bacon on toast and one huge ginormous cup of coffee what do you reckon Taff me old fruit"

"I'm a porridge man meself, I reckon eating porridge will make me more like Popeye"

"Well you look more like Pluto right now Taff you fat git, and what's your excuse for listening to Tubeway Army then"

"Oh you mean that classic group I was playing the other day on the wireless"

"On the what Taff"?

"Wireless you know isnit, the tape player thingy"

"Just get your porridge and sit down Taff bloody ell"

"Ken, he's thinking of olive oil too much"

Jock Mernie butted in with Ken in tow as always, one of these days it might be possible to have some food without pissing our sides in the process.

"What's next on the agenda then Jock? You have just had a conflab with Corporal Camilari"

"We have got weapon training and test, which is strip clean and reassemble slr, lmg, smg and the browning pistol, and then the gymnasium trapezium trainasium thingy that you have to stand up on a small platform about forty foot up and shout your name and number, Piece of piss"!

Well we all passed the weapons training which I might be being brave in saying that it was almost easy and enjoyable, in a sort of a therapeutic meditational sort of way, listening to the cold metal pieces sliding and clicking into place and the resounding thud of the mechanism when the trigger was squeezed, pretty damn calming if you ask me. The rest of the squad agreed however scouse Moran had his mind on the next task in question which was the trainasium.

"What's up scouse you look like you have seen a ghost"?

"Not ten"

"Oh right then you getting the brews in then"?

Corporal Camilari walks over towards us from sergeant Alfreton who was now putting all the weapons away in a land rover,
"Right you orrible bunch of good for nothings, get yourself a brew and then where are off to the next task, so I want you at the trainasium in twenty minutes"

Well that gives us about two minutes to walk over to the table where the flask is at the other side of the training field, get a brew then five minutes to peg it up to the trainasium which was about two hundred foot away. Doddle!

"Good brew that Scouse, have you heard how scouse Roberts Is In hospital"?

"Er, he's er in some like sort of a light coma which they say has to have a natural recovery, in other words no excessive brain stimulation, just a matter of time they say"

"Hmm that doesn't sound clever does it I didn't realise that log hit him that hard"   I said

"Well I always said he needed a good thump on the bonce, he will probably wake up with more brain cells than what he had before"!

"How many will that be then five "?

"Yeah five or six you comedian, come on let's get down to the trainasium trapezium thingy"

"Right men up that hill there last one back gets twenty"

Bloody ell we thought that's all we need before testing our stability on a forty foot high climbing frame, so off we went on a jolly jog up the hill and down again.

"Keep runnin keep running keep running keep running"

Corporal Camilari's trademark words of enthusiasm bellowed out for the last five hundred yards.

"Private White twenty press ups if you don't mind, Scouse, up you go top of the platform, stand up and shout out name rank and number and wait for my command, understood, come on white I said twenty not twelve".

Scouse made his way over to the trainasium gingerly like and without confidence and started to climb the lower part of the framework. He climbed upwards and kept looking down, not exactly the best recipe for success but continued nevertheless. Scouse was now on the fourth set of bars out of ten, he slowed his movements down and stopped, no head movements no limb movements, a human statue stood on two bars and holding onto one. A few moments were allowed to pass whilst we shouted up comments of encouragement but they were not having any effect scouse would not move, He slowly wrapped his right arm around one of the bars and curled it around the corner of another and pulled himself in, he was going nowhere.

By this time the decision was made by Sergeant Hunter and Corporal Camilari to climb up and see if they could coax him anywhere up or down. We could tell that the NCOs had done this many a time before as they climbed up and faced the height frightened soldier. We could not hear what they were saying to scouse however within minutes scouse was moving ever so slowly inch by inch bar by bar, downwards towards the ground. Scouse walked away from the frame with his head down and looking sullen and annoyed with himself.

"Right scouse go and get a brew and ten minutes out, then watch your mates do it, that might give you a bit of confidence to try again you are lucky the Captain isn't here or he would just fail you without giving you a second chance, ok Jock Mernie get up there"

Although scouse watched us all do the test and pass he decided not to try again and gave Sergeant Hunter no choice but to send him home, PVR

We were taken for a class room lesson on first aid and scouse went to pack his stuff have a ciggy and remove himself from the barracks.

"Volunteer please, well done that man, name? Come on man, come up come up"

Staff Sergeant Hoollahan was in good form today, he was a strange sort but very funny, I think from Devon somewhere with a very posh accent. He sported a huge farmers moustache, like a country gent perhaps, or a lord of some manor or a landlord of a proper good old fashioned public house that sold real beer not the watered down NAAFI crap that was sold here. His voice had a lisp and seemed to echo after every base tone probably from giving speeches after the local hunt.

"White. Staff Sergeant, my names White"

"Right Chalky, get yourself down on the floor and pretend you are injured, come on man, be sharp, stop faffing about you messer. Ok listen in, Chalky here has had his elbow shot to pieces, no arm in that".

Staff sergeant Hoolahan produced a double bass tommy gun laugh at his own unfunny joke which seemed to last about two minutes, which inadvertently forced us to break into a fit of hysterics

"So he needs a bandage, now it is an open wound but no bones protruding so look in and I will show you how to correctly place the bandage over the wound and where to place the patient to recover".

So now we know how to put a bandage on a limb and make a sling out of a scrim scarf , really handy if you have a wound that needs supporting, we all looked at each other in appreciation of our newly gained rgn qualifications and were wondering where our breast pocket watch was. The end of the lesson came and we were issued with a free bandage to practice with.

By the time we had done some parade drill and twenty minutes pt and swimming lessons it was time for scran again, and we were told to fill up as the big run is the day after. It must have been the first night we could actually get to sleep at ten o clock, and I presume that was allowed for us to get some recuperation.

Yorkshire.

Harrogate was a town that most people thought was fairly wealthy and posh and crime free, but in amongst the millionaires were villains, drug lords, cigarette smugglers and gangsters galore.

Michael Consallo was of Italian descent and was a big fish in "Family business" with several different interests all around Yorkshire, all respectable and legal of a fashion, the man was a well-known figure in society, very frequently having barbeques and dinner events in his country mansion just on the outskirts of Knaresborough, always invited were high ranking officials, MP's, investment bankers, and other influential members of the local community.

It was four in the afternoon and Michael was walking through the two barns to the side of the main building where he lived, to meet his fifteen year old daughter Alana who was on her way back from a horse ride on the forty four acre estate. One of the workers, a butler, came rushing to find him and inform him that there was a phone call from his solicitor, confidant and consigierlarie Marcus Haig.

Marcus Haig had met Michael Consallo ten years ago whilst working for Massingbourne and Co of Harrogate one of the biggest and best law firms in the UK, a private company only affordable by the rich and famous.

Michael had poached Marcus and asked him to be his personal solicitor for a massive salary, and of course to Marcus this was an offer he could not refuse. One of the primary advantages of having someone like Marcus was to receive all information about the family business as soon as it happened from the assorted companies and deal with any problems on paper first if possible then submit the plan to his Skipper.

Michael picked up the phone in the stable but was sure he had asked for no distractions while he tried to spend some time with his daughter while she was on school holidays.

"Sorry to bother you Michael, it's about the shell company that is being used to buy the commercial half of the Lincoln docklands, there is another company sniffing around and trying to outbid us even though we have won the rights to buy through your contacts in the council".

"Where and how much has the bid gone to, which authority"?

"Er I'm not sure which authority Michael but the bid is fourteen point six million, which I don't need to remind you is one point two million more than your shell companies bid"

"Yeah ok: Marcus, see if you can dig any information out that you can, I'll speak to my people"

"Alana come here my darling, did you have a good horse ride?" Michael hugged his daughter with love and affection and continued to ask her about everything she had done in the last three weeks, which would be quite a lot as the private boarding school that she went to was approximately fifty miles away, a bit too far for a daily visit even in the Bentley. Whilst listening to Alana, Michael thought that he would ring his associate in ten minutes, that would give him time to make a polite excuse to his Daughter that he had a few business matters to conclude on the phone and it would be good if she had lunch with her mother while he was talking to the private detective that he knew.

The private detective had many contacts, not only in the local council, he knew just about all of the best accountants in Yorkshire and he knew one of them would know something. Time to call in a favour.

Michael was also wondering why someone was deliberately making this deal awkward for him, this had not happened before, even when he was buying houses in Harrogate.

Parachute Regiment Training Depo

The twenty mile tab went well and for a change there were no injuries worth a mention, just Andy White moaning about his Bergen strap breaking and having to stop to repair it with a spare boot lace which put a cut in his shoulder where it rubbed through the dpm smock. The last test and everybody passed, well all seven of us anyway. Tomorrow we would get shipped out to Jump training. All this hard work just for a piece of red cloth and the right to jump out of a perfectly serviceable plane.

The night passed and we had a fairly good sleep as we were all pissed as farts. Sergeant Hunter and the two Corporals had brought a load of beers in for the celebration of passing basic training, and everybody indulged only because we knew that the only detail for the day after was a debrief and move out.

After breakfast the seven of us were led to an opening near the assault course, lined up and unceremoniously presented with our trophies' for best shot, best sports person and best overall student.

"That's it lad's game over, just the jumping to do now" I said to Taff.

"I think not boyo, look over yonder, there's trouble brewing I tell you trouble so there is"

Taff pointed over to the staff accommodation in a mini stance and arm out, hand open and upright in proper pointing mode.

"What's going on boys"

Jock Mernie came over and followed Taff's stretched out hand and saw what looked like Captain Macintosh and another major and two other men dressed in suits and boots, and they had just started walking towards us. Sergeant Hunter asked Corporal Camilari to go over and see what they wanted before they got here.

Corporal Camilari ran off to see if he could find out what the officers wanted and returned with orders for sergeant hunter.

Sergeant Hunter barked out in his deeply grained voice

"Right listen in men,   Taff Lewis, Jock Mernie and you Wealan off to the debrief room in hq block, the rest of you dismiss and get yourselves off to town or go home for the weekend do what you want."

The debrief room was the cleanest, newest and poshest room we had seen in the whole barracks.

There was a tea urn on a table in one corner with best china cups and saucers with a very ornate design on them, brown and white sugar cubes were decorating a shallow bowl, there was a large serving plate full of assorted quality biscuits which looked like they must have been purchased from Harrods.

Four Chesterfields filled the left corner of the room facing a wall with a full size projector screen filling it.

The velvet curtains edged the windows and had a one foot wide tie back colour coded and blended to the same colour as the carpet.

There were several paintings on the wall amongst the shields and emblems of different regiments and corps. There was even a box of cigars on a mahogany coloured desk at the other side of the room.

"Bloody 'ell, are we in the right room"?   I asked the others,

"Ken, are we in the Buckingham Palace"

The door opened and disturbed our astonished glare at each other.

"Ok Taff, Jock and you Wipples are going to listen to the two Gentlemen who will come in with Major Forrester, sit down in those brown leather things over there and make yourself comfortable until I shout sit up got it". Corporal Camilari instructed

Moments later

"Sit up" which basically meant sit to attention as there was an officer in the room.

"At ease men, get yourself a cup of tea and a biscuit, make yourself comfortable"

Jock, Taff and me sat down again and sipped our tea holding our cups in a piss take way with the little finger adrift from the cup waiving in mid-air at each other, and wondered what all this was about.

"Good Afternoon gentlemen, my name is Major Forrester and I have come from London today to speak to you three about certain opportunities made available by this government in the intelligence corps. My task is to oversee recruitment and Initialise training for a special operations force we have set up to prevent and deal with certain criminal activity.

This Gentleman to my left is Captain Black he will explain in full what we are about to offer you as a career. Captain Black".

"Thank you Major. Gentlemen let me tell you briefly what I do. I spend some of my time at my office in Whitehall and the MI5 headquarters in London and at other locations in the United Kingdom gathering and collating information for the recruitment of people who have particular skills that we need in a new special operations unit called SOK 7.

SOK 7 is a small task force containing approximately forty members. They have been recruited from different Regiments and corps of the British Army. We specialise in preventing kidnap and extortion, hence the name SOK, Special Operations Kidnap.

We need people who have shown particular strengths in fitness, creativity, intelligence, ingenuity, stamina and resilience, we have two more recruits to see who are currently at Royal Marines training centre Lympstone Devon who we hope will listen to us, any questions so far? No; good.

If you take this position you will undergo fifteen months training held at different organizations all over the world. You will spend five months anti-terrorist training at GSG9 headquarters in Germany, three months intel training at Cia headquarters in Langley USA, three months studying politics, Law and languages at Oxford university, you will be taught in self-defence up to black belt fourth dan aikido by the best instructor in Europe.

After the fifteen months training you will have more superior knowledge than any soldier in the British army, you will be taught how to sleep with one eye open, how to shadow a suspect without being seen and how to speak in five different languages. Then to finish off you will have explosives and munitions training at Hereford. Oh and there is the added benefit of having diplomatic status wherever you go"

The tea went cold while we were listening to all that gubbins, our mouths gaped in disbelief by the offer that was on the table, given by an Armani suited and booted man who spent most of his time behind a desk and a Major who we had never seen before   The silence was broken by Taff biting into a toffee coated hob nob type biscuit,   and then he looked at us slightly lifting his arms and shoulders in a "I don't know fashion"

"You have been recommended to us by your NCOs who were approached last year to look out for recruits with your skills, but have only just now come across anybody who would be a suitable candidate.   You will need some time to think it over I presume, we shall return in 1 hour. If you accept you will be allowed some Christmas leave and after that you will not see your family for approximately eighteen months, any questions, no good, see you in one hour"!

The two intelligence people from SOK 7 disappeared through the door knowing what the answer would be and left us to polish off the Harrods biscuits and cat pea tea.

"Bloody ell lads I feel like a regular James Bond"
 "Eye, and I feel like Doctor bloody No"
   "What do you reckon Taff"?
 "I reckon's I need a cup of tea I do, it's the excitement of it all I'm not sure I can cope"

      Taff was of course being sarcastic, he loved all this spy stuff, could not wait to get to the CIA headquarters Jock and I could see it in his eyes. I did a pretty useless impression of Bruce lee messing about in jest,   skitting the fact that we would be taught aikido right up to black belt and above, wicked!

  "Ken, what's Diplomatic status mean"
 "It means Jock, that even you will be untouchable where ever you go,

"Shit I don't believe this is happening, no but Yeah, no, what about er, no"

I could not manage to complete a whole sentence being still under shock and full of excitement.

By the time we had drunk all the tea and most of the coffee   the hour was nearly up and almost to the second the two majors reappeared and demanded the nod.

"Congratulations gentlemen you have decided to join a unique special forces unit, and I must stress that this information must be kept completely classified as we are in fact a unit that has no publicity due to the secrecy of our missions, therefore we have had your kit from your rooms packed and put into bags and there will be a hire car waiting outside the barracks for each of you.   You cannot see your` companions from your training here again, orders will be forwarded to you at your addresses. Major Forrester and I will see you after Christmas".

The door opened and off they went, before the door could shut Sergeant Hunter and corporal Camilari walked in.

"Not so fast boys,   we just need a quick word before you disappear sit ye down you bunch of good for nothing miscreants"

Sergeant Hunter had a particular way with words and he always bellowed the sound in a deep way a bit like Rod Stewart.

"Here we have some prizes for the three stooges,   for you Taff,   the medallion for best recruit,   you Jock,   a medallion for fittest ,   and last but not least Wealip from Chorley the medallion for the best shot, make sure you pin it on your pinny before you go and play spies,   well done lads be seeing ya"

Corporal Camilari was just about to follow,

"Corporal Cheers"

I hoped this would portray my thanks for his expert tuition.

"I'm not going yet you big girls blouse, follow me and I'll take you to the gate and show you where your cars are"

"Corporal er how is scouse Roberts after that bump on the head"?

"Still in a coma but stable, he'll come round I'm sure, did Captain Black tell you anything about what he wants you for"?

"Yeah"

"Oh right big secret then is it"?

"Yeah"

"Bloody ell you prick I've signed the official secrets act more times than you have had jam doughnuts. If it's special ops they were here last year but we couldn't recommend anyone. So it is them is it, well, best of luck boys, I'm sure you will have a good time, what do they do exactly"?

"Special operations Corporal"!

"Ok smartarse, there are your cars parked outside the gate, if you go and see Corporal Harrison in the gate house he will give you the keys, I'll see you in the Klondike"

We didn't really know what that meant but we were hoping it meant good luck.

The CONSALLO OFFICE.

Karl Tremane was sifting through some accounts of a regular customer and didn't find anything untoward, he was just checking that none of his genuine clients had not become non genuine clients, in other words had become money launderers for some Mafia underlord which is what he had seen before many a time.   He passed them on to his assistant who also checked and double checked for irregularities.

"Helen I'm looking for someone who deals in odd properties, large stuff, where are the newest lists of sealed bids for ex council owned properties do you know"?

"Karl I'll have to go down to Harrogate property office and see my friend again, the list we had was accidentally thrown away, she nearly got into trouble last time as well"

"Oh right, here have some money take her out for lunch or something"

"Karl, there is a hundred pounds here"

"Yeah, try that Italian on the main street, there are no prices on the menu, it must be free, you can put the money in your pocket then"

Helen knew the place well. She had been before and the real reason the menu had no prices was that if you needed to know prices before you ordered then you could not afford to be there. So it was a chicken salad in the nearest pub called the Crown, and forty quid each for personal shopping items.

Helen sat down and waited for her friend who worked for the council on a part time basis but was the most qualified person there so was trusted with information that others were not, the sort of information that could change a million pound deal in minutes. It was amongst this information Helen hoped would be the answer to Karl's puzzle, and so would get a bonus off Michael Consallo.

"Helen darling how are you, how long has it been?

 "Two months too long I think Rebecca, how are you, can I get you a drink"?

   "Yes please, dry white wine if you don't mind and what information are you after this time then"?

   "Surely we must talk about the gossip first, did your cousin marry that married man?
Karl has given me a hundred quid this time shall we split it again., He's after a name, somebody who has put a bid in on the Lincoln docklands deal and upset the whole contract which was supposed to be a closed bidding, and we knew the other bidders or so we thought",

   "Hmm the plot thickens then does it, let me have a look tomorrow morning the boss isn't in the morning so I can look in the filing cabinets for the names and addresses, yes she did marry him and they came back off honeymoon split up for a week and now they are back together again just about, oh I don't know something to do with one of his ex's you know how it is."

Helen and Rebecca continued to gossip and were eating their lunch for about three hours and of course were late getting back to their respective employers.
Karl asked Helen if her friend knew anything but for now the answer could only be she will have a look.

   "Right so that could be a few days then, we had better look at the new companies listed on the new companies register, I know somebody at the offices in Leeds, it's got to be a new company or I would have heard of the bid on the grapevine before now"

Karl was intrigued by the audacity of the company involved and where they were from, all local companies would only get the chance to offer a price if they could prove that they had the money and that the development would benefit the local community as in creating as many jobs as possible, and this deal would create about five thousand jobs so the deal might not be given to the highest offer but more the best offer that suited the council and perhaps the one that came with a wad of cash for the Council property manager. Karl thought he had access to all the bidders' information right up till this latest spanner in the works. Karl was stretching all his contacts and pulling all his favours in, not just for Michael Consallo but because now it was ever so slightly personal, how dare someone invade his county and not leave their calling card.

TRAINING CAMP GATES

"Bloody ell lads three Escort ghia's alloys and everything, Wicked",

"Ken, mine's got leather trim",

"What's yours like Taff"?

"Looks like it's got a decent enough wireless in it, at least I can play my Gary Numan tape isn't it boyo"

We all said our goodbye's and followed each other out of the vicinity of the camp and locate the nearest motorway and head North West, North and Wales. All I could think about was how was I going to explain to my family and friends the fact that I have come home on leave from basic training with a brand new car, not the normal thing to do for a recently passed basic training squaddie. My Mum would say something along the words of why do you need a car if you are travelling all over the world? And my mates would say I could have bought a decent car? Even if I admitted it was a hire car they would say it was a bit extravagant, never happy some people

The drive home was a good one with only one piss stop, that was just like a pit stop but there was no changing of tyres, just a quick brew which cost a fortune and toilet stop and then back on the road.

Back at home already, it didn't seem like five minutes ago that I was here, but I was away long enough for my bedroom to be decorated and recarpeted and be in a position to be awaiting new furniture, I'm sure that was done so that I couldn't say is my room just as I left it.

What I found most difficult was the fact that I had to explain to everyone why I had to be away for another eighteen months and couldn't tell people where I was and who with, the only person I told where was my Mum, and that was America and Germany, oh and my cousin. Who had inadvertently set me up on a blind date with some girl that was a friend of his, and they were going out tonight so I had to get my best togs on and dig the grave, shave, for those that don't talk Wealan rhyming slang.

I had My favourite tea which was three ham salad barmcakes spent some time with my Mum telling her about stuff in basic training and how much fun it was.

My blind date was fairly good looking, not the normal type I go for but slim, attractive, hair right down to her waist and would definitely do for the short time I was home, and I did explain to her that I wouldn't be around for about a long time possibly two years and she wasn't bothered, but I could not see a full time relationship being on the cards for more than a few months and would expect a dear John letter soon enough. So we got absolutely sloshed and had food and a coffee and that was that!

The holiday break seemed to pass really quickly and the town I left to serve the Queen had not changed at all, in fact it looked even more depressing than it did before. Everything looked grey and miserable, all the people walked round with such sad faces, I did not miss this place, it bored me to tears.

The next day there was a knock on the door and the postie handed me a letter and a copy book to sign on. It was a letter to me, a brown envelope had the words, "On her Majesties service stamped on the back of it, I thought this looks interesting, maybe its offer to join the royal navy or the air force, hmm I think not. It was orders from Major Black, or at least it was signed Black.

Seventh of January Return hire car to Manchester airport before eleven hundred hours, get on the plane to Stanstead airport, Itinerary below.

Then make way to Carlton hotel two miles from the airport and await further instructions from the reception desk.
Pack smart casual clothes, toilet bag etc
Shaving facial hair is not required
Bring driving license and passport if held.
Bloody ell I thought no shaving, that's alright but however I was gutted that I had to give the car back, I was just getting used to it.

I'll have to get on another of these flights that's two women who I'm sure were trying to chat me up, and the coffee was actually fairly drinkable, although it did cost one pound, and maybe I'll get to join the mile high club yet!
There were no customs as such just a quick walk through a metal detector to which I set off with my belt buckle, I eventually ended up at the taxi rank and waited for a taxi, the driver was a cheerful chappy he kept telling jokes which just were not funny but he kept smiling nevertheless.

The Carlton hotel was pretty luxurious, there were plants in the reception that were six feet high and revolving glass doors with ornate coloured patterns draping the sides of the glass which had a slight green tint to them.

The reception area or lounge area as it was called had beautiful two tone brown leather armchairs with glass coffee tables in the same colour as the doors. There was a desk in one corner of the reception area which had a very important person look and feel about it, a marble top was decorated with a gold cigar box and some of those cigarette holders that actors from the thirties and forties used and of course the Financial Times was there in black and white and pink perfectly folded to reveal the front page headlines.

Behind the desk stood the concierge. If I needed anything he looked like the man to get it.

I walked over to the bar and was about to order a drink of latte from the delightful looking lady behind the bar,

"Happy new year Wealtrim"!

"Oh no, Taff Lewis how are you pal, and what the bloody ell is that slug doing under your nose, do you want some glue to stop it falling off ? You must have got the letter about no shaving as well then did you"?

"Yes I thought I'd take advantage of the letter I got stating that shaving wasn't necessary and by the way I had been told that I look like Tom Sellick from Magnum"

"Well I think not, more like Bill or Ben, one of the flower pot men, get the beers in then"

Three beers later we were thinking that our new bosses might want us to do something which requires a little soberness but after the fourth beer we had forget about the concern and a disturbance from the triple glazing revolving door made our heads turn and there he was, the third musketeer,

"Jock I think you are the first person this year to walk through those doors making more noise than Man United fans in the final"

"Bloody Sassenach door, see that Ken the thing nearly mashed ma heid, how is everybody then,"?

"We're half pissed by the way, how are you"?

"I'm completely judge sober as yet, but still managed to stagger through that doorway and fall over my kitbag. Get me a Whisky immediately!"

About a half an hour later Jock noticed this tall man walk into the hotel and hook into reception, and he also noticed him look around and noticed him look three or four times at me.

"Here Wealtrim see that bloke over there he's giving you the eye do you know him",

"Shit he's walking over here is there going to be a rumpus here or what"?

I was looking at the man and could swear blind I've seen him before but was too drunk to remember where.

"It's Paul isn't it?"

"Yeah, and I'm totally embarrassed because I know I've seen you before but my memory has been affected by some light intoxication, perhaps you can enlighten me"!

"Yes My name is O'Leary, Conall O'Leary,"

I could just overhear Taff whispering into Jock's ear

"My name is Bond, James Bond with a girly giggle in each other's ear.

"Shut it will you I'm trying to concentrate on where I know Conall from."

"We met on the train down to basic training, you were going to the Para's and I was going to Lympstone"

"Ah the penny has dropped at last, you were sent here by Major Black then"

"Yeah that's right"

"Good it's your round pull up a stool,   Lads meet Conall."

As the party was in full swing we were thinking of asking the concierge to organize some female companions for us but I don't think we had enough money on us they would have been expensive here if the price of the drinks were to be an indication of the price of everything else.

"Hey Conall, was there not anybody else from Lympstone I'm sure Major Black said to us that there was to be two coming"?
"Ah yes that would be Andy Elphick, he ain't coming now he's chickened out didn't want to be away from his fiancé who I think is pregnant or so he said."

"Right looks like you are the fourth musketeer then"

There was a roar of laughter and joke after joke and piss take after piss take we could not even have a drink without being ripped into by one another.

One of the hotel porters came over with what seemed like an empty tray which was fairly small as far as trays go, and I thought to myself is there a bill on it or summat, I thought we had been paying as we go along,

"Excuse me Sir's is there a Hamish Mernie amongst you"?

"Hamish! Ere Jock is that you Hamish"

Jock replied in a drunken stupor dribble,

"Eye that's ma name dinna wear it oot ya wee poof"

Jock was passed the piece of A5 conqueror cream coloured paper with the hotels crest parched in the top right hand corner.

"A message sir"

"Cheers r kid"

Again, spoken with inerberance and dribble of a man half cut with alcohol.

"I canna read it man, ken the scribblings too wee"

"Bloody ell give us it here"

I snatched the note off Jock and began to read.

"Ay up lads we are off to Germany, listen. Your advanced concentrated training will begin the day after tomorrow at the GSG9 headquarters in Germany, collect tickets from hotel reception.

"Shit, so we have to work with a load of boxheads who don't know their arse from their elbow in boxhead land an all"? "Yep looks like it pal, must be cheap beer over there anyways" Get em in Jock, your round"

"Ken, will you stop calling me round".

CONSALLO OFFICE

Michael made his evening walk through his gardens and thought of going to Lincoln to sort out this deal and make sure he didn't lose it to foreigners. He was curious as to why they wanted this property and land so much because his bid was a premium one anyway. Michael asked his wife when their daughter Alana was going back to school and she told him it was in two days' time. Michael thought he could take her back in a helicopter and then go on to Lincoln for a few days. With the information he was given by his trusted specialist Karl, Michael thought it prudent to employ his temporary part time bodyguard, an ex-royal bodyguard to accompany him in Lincoln. Michael made the call but unfortunately the bodyguard was abroad on a job for someone else, ah what the hell I'll go on my own Michael said to himself.

Michael Consallo landed his Belle Jet Ranger helicopter at Lincoln golf club, with which he had an agreement with, he sponsored the golf shop and in return he had free helicopter parking,

"Good afternoon Mr Consallo how are you today"?

The golf club porter greeted Michael and took his booking for a room with a view for two nights and ordered two other porters to retrieve Michael's luggage from the helicopter and take it to his room. The golf club only had six rooms to rent, but they were of a particular quality and had enough space for him to do office work and look over the beautiful and tranquil forty acre golf course.

The hotel room telephone rang, it was the porter at reception asking if he was available for a game of golf with a business man who was visiting the area, this was a regular occurrence for Michael when he was here, he had on several occasions played with strangers just to get out on the green and practice the sport that gave him exercise. Michael told the porter he would be down in five minutes and meet him in the bar.

Michael walked out of the lift and was walking towards the bar when the porter joined him purely out of hotel etiquette to introduce him to his opponent.

"Hello again Sir, can I introduce Michael Consallo, Michael may I Introduce Goran Kolorov"

both men shook hands said their greetings and made their way to the first hole, whilst chatting away politely to each other they both realised they had a lot in common, and this was the fact that they both had commercial property companies and they both bought large concerns. The pair were at the fourteenth hole when Michael wondered if he should mention the Lincoln docks deal, maybe this fella had knowledge of who managed to get past the red tape and tender the higher bid in at the council.

"Good shot Goran, by the way I don't suppose you have dealt with any local councils in any deals of yours recently have you "?

"I have not no, my deals are with a large accountancy firm who just take a hefty commission and all I do is sign a cheque, it gives me time to, well play golf "

"And the accountancy firm, would they have dealings with any council property sales"?

"I wouldn't know how they do the deals or who with, I just give them money",

"You must trust them"

"Yes, they are from the same country as me and the rules of that country are that if you betray a fellow countryman in a business deal there will be dire consequences, and of course they are making lots of money for the both of us"

"Yes of course; was there a bet on this game?"
"Perhaps the next, I will buy you dinner if you win".

WEST GERMANY. (K-TEAM)

Gsg9 headquarters was like a fortress with its own airfield training area and close quarter battle housing estate, there were other individual buildings which had a prison like appearance with bars across the windows and then there was a completely modern building with a glass fronted wall, solar panels on the roof and in the car, park were six of the biggest Audi's I have ever seen.

"Here Taff what do you reckon of those beasts over there "?

"Bloody German crap isn't it, wouldn't last five minutes driving up the Snowdon would it boyo"!

I looked at Jock and Conall, they looked at me and we all looked at Taff, in disbelief,

"Pray what vehicle would have superlative design, ultimate reliability and sheer roar as to match what you see there,   I think you have a case of epic misinterpretation of the quality of those vehicles young fella mi lad".

"I'm telling you German crap it is, you'll see, you can't beat a good old Ford Cortina"

"Ken, you aren't feeling well man"

Amongst the laughter there were shaking of heads and comments to the effect of has he had his tablet today?

"Stick to map reading Taff."

We had been dropped off by a mini bus which had met us at the airport, we did ask how much it was even though we didn't see any meter, but the driver said in an American accent

"It has already been taken care of Sir"

"Bloody ell, you are American"?

"Er no, I'm certainly not some Yo big daft dozy Yank. I am Canadian actually, I work here"

"Here meaning there"?

I pointed to the mass of buildings, old aircrafts and other training obstacles that were in front of us all, puzzled as to why a Canadian was here.

"So how come you are on taxi driving duties"

"Well I double up as an explosives instructor, and if I am not mistaken I am giving you a lesson tomorrow after your German language lesson".

There is your Boss, Major Black, he will want to show you around and where you are going to live for the next five months"

Conall, Jock, Taff and I walked over towards Major Black who was dressed casual in Levi jeans and a shirt that could have resembled a Ben Sherman, and training shoes on his feet.

"Welcome chaps, come on then let's be having you, while we are walking over to your accommodation I can inform you that during your time here and throughout your career in Sok 7, there will be a need to blend in and not look like a policeman or a squaddie, as one or two of you do now, let your hair grow and your beard, if you want start wearing smarter clothes when you are out, a bit more trendy perhaps, you will have a company credit card to use with limits gentlemen !, I will also need your passports and driving licences, they will be sent to the relevant departments for diplomatic marking, and your salary has increased with immediate effect."

"What to Sir "?

"Enough, Jock, enough. By the way don't call me Sir, my first name is Roger, and I will call you what you want".

"Well you can call Taff as much as you want he deserves it the daft welsh bugger"

"You are a funny guy wealtrim, that's why I'm gonna kill you last".

The humour was still about us although we hadn't heard much inanity from the Irish Connal we knew that when the time came he would be flourishing fluent Gaelic nonsense and have us all rolling about the floor with uncontrollable stitch wrenching movements, but for now all about us was serious, what with hand to hand combat training with alternative weapon introduction first thing tomorrow morning, then some sort of pt training till lunch, and the afternoon instruction was on explosives and pyrotechnics then as if that wasn't enough, there was urban chase, which was a term for learning to follow someone without being spotted and how to go walkabout without being spotted yourself, all good stuff ! Oh and then apparently we are to be taught how to sleep with one eye open. And speak German.

"So lads you have this block all to yourselves, one ensuite room each a rest room a library come study, and usual washing facilities room and that's about it, er one last thing no women at all in camp grounds , see you all at six thirty sharp".

"Bugger, we'll have to go out then, there must be some women out there somewhere"?

"Ken there's a club called Rainbow's in the nearest town "!

Jock's ears picked up as soon as women were mentioned he did think of himself as a bit of a ladies man, although all the stories he told us of his conquests were slightly exaggerated we thought ; and boring.
Roger Black came in our living block at Six fifteen and made sure that we weren't either drunk or incapable.

"Right lads make sure you all get good food at breakfast you have a busy day ahead and do me a favour see if you can lamp one on the instructor he's a Pratt"

Jock was nearest to Roger so he replied in a posh university type voice

"Roger, "

Meaning ok in radio telephony vocabulary and of course the first name of our mentor, an attempt at humour no doubt, Roger didn't laugh but did raise his eyebrows and glanced at the rest of us in dismay.

"See that block over there gents, that's where you need to be in pt kit at eight o clock and I will see you later on".

The instructor was about five feet ten and strangely enough had blonde hair and a blonde moustache, he wasn't massively built but athletic, and had a strong German twang in his speech, every ten words spoken in English had three words spoken in German and his sentences seemed to be backwards but understandable.

"Please here sit, und I need three volunteers"

Jock Connal and Taff stood up and walked over to the mat where the instructor was stood.

"You three stand in circle and when I say go attack me, GO"   all at once, go!

Jock ran straight in fists flying and Connal and Taff followed ,   Jock threw his right arm towards the instructors face expecting it to make contact with at least a bone somewhere, but no, the instructor's face pulled sideways and with a lightning movement grabbed Jock's hand and bent it ninety degrees with the slightest of force then with his other hand grabbed Jocks elbow pushing it upwards, then using Jock's weight and motion forced him into the path of Taff who was by now trying some sort of kickboxing move with one leg in the air aimed towards the instructor.

The instructor still had hold of Jock's hand and elbow and so directed him into the path of Taff's Knee, the one knee that was stabilizing Taff.

Jock ended up head butting Taff's knee with the same force of motion and speed that he tried to attack the instructor with, the result was Taff and Jock in a pile on the floor moaning and groaning and in bits, Connal ran towards the instructor wanting revenge, his height must gain an advantage in a frontal assault which both parties knew and presumed that a simple overhead punch would get through so he attempted to thrust his arm in a roundhouse movement which would have normally floored an elephant, but the instructor parried the blow and twisted and locked Connals arm leaving his hand to push him off balance and onto the pile of bodies on the floor. Well that was a fair demonstration of self defence I thought to myself.

The instructor introduced himself as Sense Oregon,   and he informed us that he had lived and learnt skills in Korea and Thailand over a fifteen year period and was now employed by the German government and the American government and spent an equal time throughout the year at Langley USA and the rest here in Germany, so I suppose he was qualified.

"Ok please on ze mat standen sie jezt, I would like to teach you the art of hand combat. This morning we will learnen multiple assailant defence, can I have your names bitte"

What seemed like three hours was in fact one and a half hours and up to now there wasn't much blood just a few embarrassed trainees with sore muscles and limbs, how on earth can this man not be touched with four of us? Was he actually the son of Bruce lee perhaps?.

Our defence moves were getting faster and faster by the minute and our reactions were certainly lightning quick, you just don't get training like this at the local Karate centre, for instance we didn't know how important a backhanded slap to the eardrum can immobilise the assailant by simply upsetting his or hers balance, and a scrape down the assailants shin with your shoe and a stamp on the toes with a decent size ten is painful too.

CONSALLO HOUSEHOLD

Marcus Haig was preparing a portfolio of information about the mystery bidder, there was a fair amount of pages to read and the last of the pages contained a recommendation to not increase the bid but just wait and hope the council picked his shell companies bid instead of the Kolorov enterprises bid. After several days investigation Marcus had discovered that company of solicitors and accountants that made the bid were under the control of the Russian mafia headed in this country by Goran Kolorov.   The dossier also contained information on previous deals in England
That took place and who pulled out of the deals and what Marcus thought was the reason why. Some of these reasons included suspicions of blackmail and extortion or in general people being too frightened to do battle with a Russian.

Marcus was summoned to Michael Consallo's house for morning coffee and an update and talk through of the file, the weather was sunny in Knaresborough so Michael and Marcus sat outside on a veranda to the rear of the property which overlooked the Consallo grounds, the Yorkshire moors and Harrogate, a house maid served coffee and Yorkshire tea was made available but generally not taken, the tea was an idea of Michael's his way of supporting the local companies and it stood as an alternative to espresso which was almost always too strong for the women of the household.

"So Marcus what is your overall opinion of the situation at this moment in time"

   "I do know we are dealing with a villain Michael, who has endless amounts of cash available at his disposal, and also has I believe many high ranking policemen on his payroll, he has several bodyguards too, one of them, his driver has a bit of a reputation as a wrong un, apparently he stabs people with a samurai sword.   Drives around in a Jaguar as well the cheek."!

"Did you get the names of the men at the top"?

"Well yes although there are just two names that I can tell   you, one is the name of the company that deals with his transactions which is called Ivano,   a shell company similar to yours but the company is made up of highly skilled accountants and solicitors, very good at their job, in fact I wouldn't mind them working for us in another situation.   The second name that I can tell you is the man at the top who is in charge of all Uk business is Goran Kolorov , a Russian educated in England but has had regular trips to Moscow recently."

"Wait   a minute Kolorov I know that name I played golf with him last week"

"What, golf how on earth did that happen"?

"I was at the golf club last week and the porter introduced him as a golfer looking for a game as his booked opponent could not make it, bloody hell "!

"Yes I don't think the introduction was a coincidence does you Michael "? Maybe he has had you followed, or perhaps had you watched,   what did you talk about with him, anything relevant "?

"Yes everything relevant, I asked him about his property dealings and if he had any dealings with any council, and I do remember him saying he employed a company to manage everything, Maronne"!

"Michael you will have to think about this, do you really want the docklands deal"?
"Well the council hasn't accepted his bid yet have they"!

"Michael, the more I learn about this man, the more I suspect he will win the deal "

"Yes I think I will wait to see if he has managed to bribe anyone first, if not then I win legally, and I'll have a rethink then".

Michael and Marcus both supped their espresso and had refills of the Italian imported coffee, and had a few moments silence to gather thoughts.

"Dam it, bloody Russian Mafia, I've a good mind to contact my friends in Italy, Marrone!"

Marcus left happy that Michael now knew the risks of the deal, and happy that he had advised him wisely to be very cautious not only of his business but of his personal life as well.

Michael had a look at the property details which he already had from months ago, in particular the survey of the land, trying to find something out of the ordinary, anything that would attract the Russian mob, after all it was only a plot old waste land which seemed to have no importance apart from the potential of building houses where the factories were.   Michael did not see anything so made the decision to contact his commercial surveyor and ask the question.

"Hello Ronald, Michael Consallo here, sorry to bother you but I was wondering if you could do me a favour, I am trying to buy the Lincoln Docks wasteland through the Council sealed bid system, and someone has beat the system and somehow got a bid in past the rules and regs, and apparently it is a Russian Mafia type person, and I was hoping you could cast your eye over the survey for me or let me know if you think the wasteland has any other valuable reason why it should be so interesting to someone like that"?

"Yes of course Michael, I'm a little bit busy myself but I'll get someone on it right away"
"Many thanks"

Michael was walking towards the barn to look in on his daughters horse and the horse handler who he had a secret admiration for, but she was twenty five years younger than he was so it was a large gap in years for him to cope with, too much stress these young women, His thoughts were interrupted by a phone call from Marcus Haig.

"Michael I have had a friend on the phone who works for Lincoln Council, and she reckons that there has been problems in the property department, one of the chief executives is now off sick with some sort of stress disorder, and he was apparently being threatened by somebody who was going to blow his car up, the police came in and spoke to him, and he denied ringing them and made no formal complaint, He was one of the people that could have signed the acceptance of the bid from the Russian company and was one of the only people who would allow it in from outside, the sealed bid system or the invitation only bidding.

He has had to have three months off work by order of a psychiatrist apparently; the whole thing has knocked him for six. I'm not sure if this is a deal that you should be going through with Michael"   "Marrone, why is business so unpredictable, I've never had any problems like this before in the thirty years I've been in business, what's going on "?

"I think it is just a one off Michael   it must be that particular piece of land, I don't know,

"Well it's a mighty big one off,   I'll see if I can speak with anyone at the council to see how my offer is going on,   grazzi Marcus, I'll see you on Friday at the golf club cafe"

The Golf club café as it was known was a high class place where golfers, business men and other members of the same ilk frequented, mainly to talk about the different makes of golf balls and the price hike of the daily telegraph and other unimportant subjects like that, a sort of Masonic meeting where one could have a cigar in peace if one desired. Or a conflab about nothing to a potential client, coffee was served by ladies of a professional background who had been vetted and particularly picked for their outstanding résumé's which had evidence of discretion and secrecy, there were no prices on the order cards, customers just got what they wanted and their company received the invoice at the month end on an entertainment titled letter. If you had to ask how much the service was you couldn't afford to be there.

GSG9 TRAINING DEPO GERMANY

After demoralising us all with Bruce Lee training skills the self defence instructor gave us a half hour tea break and told us then to go to building four for our next lesson. We made our way to the rest room which was a plain room with a few tables and chairs, but most important of all there was a table with a tea urn on it and coffee and milk. Splendid!

"It must be your round Taff"?

"Oh is it my round then is it, shall I get the brews in then, bloody typical isnit the stupid thing is empty,"

"Ken, fill the bugger up then "

"I am trying to get the lid of it appears to be stuck doesn't it"

"Give us it here Taff, Connal can you grab the bottom of the urn and I'll turn it from the top, yep you are right there Taff it is well and truly stuck"!

"Ah all this stuff and we can't fill the bloody kettle thing up, rahh,"

"I don't suppose anyone has any mole grips on them have they"

"Yes Taff I've got three spanners and a hammer as well in my back pocket you daft sod, come on your not telling me that four of us can't get the lid of this thing, by the time we get it filled up and boiled it will be time to go"

"Here Jock try my belt around the top of it as a sort of oil filter wrench type thing"
"It's not a car! Wealtrim!!

"Just a minute why don't you try picking it up and lightly banging the top of it on the edge of the table   like you would a jam jar when the lid is stuck or too tight"

"Right hang on a min   Yes!!

 At last movement in the lid and it's off,

 "Right get it filled up someone"   everybody want sugar except me then "?

"Are you sure you know how to make a cup of tea weals "?

"You what pal "?

"Well the last one you made was a bit,   well,   Wish washy"!

"Wish washy, what are you talking about Taff"?

"It tasted like you hadn't done it right"

"bloody ell Taff if I'd known you were going to be a fussy twat I would have read the tea making manual beforehand, Jock what was that last brew like I made"?

"Ken, it was a bit wish washy "!

"You see Weals what you have to do is put the tea bag in the water, then stir it thirty two times clockwise and twice anti clockwise, unless you are in the southern hemisphere, then it is thirty one times anti clockwise and three times clockwise and then leave the bag in for two minutes depending on the coriolis force of the hemisphere you are in, for instance higher the force the less time in the cup, and lower force longer time in the cup, the result : a damn fine cup of tea"!

"Shit, bloody ell, I didn't realise you had to have a PHD in Meteorology to brew up"!

"Well you don't, it just gets rid of the wish washy taste isnit, that's what you do"

"Boyo!"

Building four contained several separate rooms each with different articles of household comfort items such as settee's, tables and kitchen units. These rooms were to be used for indoor assailant prevention techniques using any available household items as weapons.

The best I found was a rolled up glossy magazine used like a batton in an arm extension sort of makeshift sword baseball bat club thing, which if rolled up the correct way would slice up the opponents skin with the sharp edges of the paper when shoved in his or hers big nose.

HEATHROW AIRPORT.

Roger Black and Alan Forrester walked off the privately chartered plane at Heathrow airport, both with attaché briefcases in their left hand.   Everybody says you can tell a military trained person by the fact he or she carries objects in the left hand only. The reason for this might be that it allows the right hand free to hold a cigar or shake someone's hand or salute a superior officer or even smack someone in the face who is asking stupid questions!
So all squaddies park their shit in their left hand.

A limousine took the important diplomatic pair to a hotel not far from the airport where a meeting was to take place, a meeting between very high security personnel, people with knowledge of political crimes and terrorism, and other serious threats against the flag and people of the United Kingdom.
The meeting participants were intelligence officer at CI5 Adrian Woodford, the operations commander from GSG9 Hans Gruber, Roger Black, Alan Forrester and a government representative from Whitehall Henri Seles, who was French and on a long term attachment from

Interpol. All parties would be present at the meeting. The smallest conference room at the hotel was booked six hours previously and a chef was employed to be on standby just in case the meeting was to last more than a few hours.

Roger Black flashed his ID card at the hotel receptionist and very quickly the young lady behind the desk noticed the red capital letter D and reacted by nodding her head at him and immediately picking up the phone to get assistance from the staff rest room.

"Sir, if you would like to follow the porters, they will escort you to the conference room and I believe three other gentlemen are waiting for you"

"Ok thank you"

The double door was pushed open by one of the porters and held open to let the three men in. Both porters walked off with a ten pounds tip each.
All the men stood up to meet and greet each other, most had met before and were used to the protocol, all brief cases were opened and folders and dossiers were put on the table that they were sat around. Henri was first to speak.

"Gentlemen here is the nasty piece of work we have been watching for approximately eighteen months, name of Goran Kolorov from Russia, from a very large family. He has brothers, cousins and sisters all in the same game, crime! They have left a path of records on extortion, burglaries, fraud and murder all over Europe. The new interest is commercial fraud, that's where the big money is and that's what he's into. Peter, your CI5 department has someone under cover I believe; have you any updates for us"?

"Yes, however he has only two weeks in place and only certain amounts of snippets worth mentioning. We are aware of blackmailing and threats made to several property executives recently, and also one or two burglaries. Two of his brothers arrived from Russia two days ago. Roger, your operative has recorded conversations of some sort of plan is that right"?

"We have collated sixteen pages of calls and information about potential crimes; however, we need more details to confirm dates and times. Unfortunately the voice recordings we have at the moment can only be construed as circumstantial evidence"

"The rest of your team"?

"Six of our operatives are undergoing training and are only half way through, four are at your department Hans, and the other two are at Langley. I have another twenty four at our hq available now and are at your service for research and intelligence gathering and operation planning, a sort of background behind the scenes team if you like".
"Excellent. Gentlemen, we need a plan!"

The men sat with heads down looking at all the information in front of them, placing all records in order and people in play, pictures were gathered and placed together in order of importance, Goran Kolorov being at the top.

Hans Gruber suggested that he would orchestrate the operational undercover work in Europe or at least in Germany and Russia, as Kolorov and his associates generally travelled through his area, and everyone agreed this would be beneficial to all.

Roger Black was trying to get all of the representatives to work at his hq to save all the hotel visits and at this point food was ordered , just a light snack of salmon salad, tea coffee and orange juice.   Adrian the CI5 rep had mentioned that the Kolorov brothers needed more surveillance than Goran as they seemed to be the soldiers of the outfit and were up to no good at all times. This task was given to the new unit set up for special operations in potential kidnap and extortion rackets, Sok 7. Normally Roger Black and Alan Forrester would not volunteer for this sort of task, but his men and women needed experience. They needed to be able to practice with their state of the art no expense spared brand new equipment while it wasn't a do or die situation, and then they could be experts when it mattered.

"Yes, I'll get my people on that Adrian,   what details have we of their current residence,"?

Hans Gruber passed Alan a folder which contained eighteen property addresses.

"Any one of these meine freunde"

"There are four brothers each of them uses all of them in no particular order. Sometimes together or alone,   there are four in England and the rest are in Europe"

"Any near your headquarters in St Augustine Hans"

"Ettringen, is a small town one hour's drive south of Bonn, they have visited a house there recently, and had several large items delivered in the last week. According to the Deutshe post they have been labelled as household items, which of course would not be what is inside them and they have been delivered from St Petersburg".

"Any information from St Petersburg as to what they are exactly"?

"Not yet Roger, however I have two Gsg9 operatives on surveillance at that location trying to trace the originator. We think possibly arms or similar."

"Henri, have you anything to input from your department"?

"Oui, I have records of shipments from Calais, several containers worth of goods, our customs officers under our instruction haven't intervened yet, purely observed and recorded, nice salmon this"!

"Yes isn't it just"

"Gentlemen, we must find out what the contents of all these parcels are, and then place an operative under cover at each location where the most parcels arrive. Roger and I have come up with a name for the mission, with everybody's approval of course, Operation Roscov ".

GSG9 HQ WEST GERMANY

"We are about to train you in the use of the flash bang grenade, smoke pellets, liquid, gas, and plastic explosives, pocket detonators, remote and mobile detonators and other interesting toys of destruction, your complete concentration and attention is required"

Connor McClellan of the Clan McClellan from in the highlands of Scotland was an ex SAS instructor of ten years who had also done time at Langley. He now resided with his French wife in a hillside three storey house in Koblenz, which was apparently one hours drive south of here, and only worked two days a week.   Another part timer!
The lesson was a little bit monotonous but not boring. I think it was just the fact that the next lesson was tactical driving that involved the use of the four litre Audi's parked outside reception with massive rear twin exhausts and a mean looking sport body kit that curved around the alloy wheels, just waiting to be woofed by us. They had to be at least five hundred horse power.

So now we were proficient at blowing things up and also had the knowledge on how to blind and shock the enemy within a small area using small items of equipment, small enough to carry in a pocket, along with other explosives to maim them with and the use of heckler and kock machine pistols that would kill anything that is left over after the pyrotechnics display.

McClellan directed us to the shooting range which was to the left of what appeared to be a workshop with technicians welding various items to land rovers that had been stripped bare of all unnecessary weight including doors and windscreens, must have been some sort of tactical assault vehicle.   The two land rovers were painted black and grey in a camouflage fashion and had two v8 engines placed in front of them, ready and waiting to be fitted.

"Come with me gents; let's see if we can't have some shooting practice with the smoke pellets and the Heck's"

The shooting range was a long room that looked very similar to a bowling alley. but without   the bowls and lanes, but in their place were channels with targets at different distances apart from each other, all painted and dressed in black with wooden rifles screwed to their wooden arms. They already had several bullet holes chips and splinters all around the frame, fragments of wood were also scattered amongst the floor of the range.
A trail of roof lights were switched on, they were plain bulbs with no covers or shades at all, this was due to a reason other than expense, perhaps it was considered a more natural light, .and better to shoot under.

"Right who is first then"?

"Go on Wealtrim,"

 Taff started off the comments of an incentive nature.

"Show em how it's done Wealtrim"

"Ken, make sure you take the safety catch off dumb-ass "
The shooting range echoed the sound of the shots and made each round sound like a double skinned click-thump, the feelgood factor triggered an adrenalin rush through my body which almost cut out the noise from my ears. Wood chips were flying in all directions; small pockets of smoke appeared from all corners of the figurine, all I could sense was sight and all I could see were holes, about three hundred of em. The instructor tapped me on the shoulder to wake me up from my moment of ecstasy as the verbal command to reload had not worked. McClellan passed me two more magazines and pointed to the next target which was further away and told me to carry on. I could see my muckers grinning away out of the corner of my eye, knowing they were itching for a go. I proceeded to unleash hell on the next three targets.

"That gentlemen, is what the Heck, is capable of" McClellan said, trying to make the statement sound a bit humorous.

Then, what was left of one of the wooden weapons screwed to the targets fell onto the floor and broke into several pieces distracting our attention and making our heads turn towards the noise and then back towards McClellan.

The door to the shooting range swung open and a blonde flat top hairstyled German wearing a blonde moustache walked in and said in a very firm tone.

"Herr McClellan, der Kommandant muchten sprecken sie mit" (The boss would like to speak to you) and gave a gentleman's nod almost like a sensei would bow to his fellow instructors after a karate lesson.

"Danke, Ich komme jezt, (I'll come now),   ok gents, I will leave you in the capable hands of my assistant Herr Munterlar, I'm off to see the boss "

Peter Munterlar walked towards us and looked at Jock.

"You are the one they call Taff the sheep yes"?

"Ken that's him there not me, ya cheeky wee bassa"

Jock was of course just informing the German that he was flattered by his comment thinking he was Welsh.

"Entshuldigung" (Excuse me)

Taff was passed the Heckler and kock and three magazines and asked politely to blat several shots in the direction of the targets on the right which as it happened were brand new and untouched by any form of bullet whatsoever.
Two minutes passed and several cheers and nods of approval amongst each other then the German spoke

"You must out with us come tonight yes beer und fraulein yes "

A quartet of yesses echoed through the shooting parlour and the German made a squiffy face which pulled his moustache up at one side and the same with one of his eyebrows, did we know what we were letting ourselves in for,   as if we were bothered.

The night started in the old town part of Cologne in a proper German pub with oak beams and flagged floors, and waitresses walking round with next to nowt on, resembling wenches from two centuries ago, carrying trays with yards of ale on them.

This was a yard long row of small glasses full of beer, usually ordered for two or three people. So we ordered four yards between seven of us, hoping that we could embarrass the Germans who were renowned lightweights in the art of drinking beer, or so we thought.

"Ere Taff pass me that pig's ear you daft Welsh bugger"

"Do you want to wear it wealtrim or drink it "?

"Connal, are you not drinking fella"?

"Eye, just admiring the blonde in the skirt over yonder pal"

"Best get some brave juice down ya then"

Peter and his two German mates had drunk more beers than all of us put together and were still compus mentus, as for us there was only Jock who was anywhere near the same state as the Germans, I think the beer was a bit strong for us mere mortals.

Connal and two of the Germans ended up going off with three blondes and were not seen again till the roll call at five thirty.

Myself, Taff and Jock all puked up on the way to breakfast and were advised to replenish the ejected mess with plenty of stodge.

Roger Black met us at breakfast and informed us that we had driver training in the Audi's after breakfast which although we had been immensely looking forward to it, our present state of physical and mental awareness was thought to be totally inadequate for the lesson.

The Major also briefed us on a live training exercise to be taking place next week in St Petersburg, covert observation and information gathering only, no interfering participation or contact, strictly training, camouflage and concealment in all the local surroundings urban style so Cefo kit was needed, in other words jeans and t- shirt plus warm Gore-Tex coats as the temperature there was minus twenty five degrees Celsius. We were to take two other German Gsg9 operatives who were to act as training officers for us and there will be a team of office surveillance staff to handle the information that we provide of the movements of the targets.

Our driving instructor was a very experienced ex royal protection officer freelancing his services to Gsg9 and the French secret service and anybody else who could pay him the going rate, which was a lot.

Robert Hardman drove the machine to its highest limits. In every gear the engine sang it's elliptic tune from the exhaust, the tyres made a rapid click click as the rubber burnt the tarmac when curved round the turns in the road, the training track was getting a pounding as the epitome of automobiles raced around it. I for one have never seen a car driven as fast in reverse as this before and then the hand brake spin to turn it around, foot brake applied, hand brake released and full throttle forward, all in a split second, demonstrating escape and evasion technique to which we were all too perfect within a few days, disregarding this lesson as we spent most of the time puking up what was drunk last night and combined with the speed and rapid steering movements of the Audi, severe travel sickness ensued.

We all relaxed in the afternoon to another German language lesson and several brufen tablets with diabolically mediocre coffee, the perfect recipe for a hangover we were told by the two Germans who inflicted this sickness upon us.

"Vielen danke fur ihre helfe you daft deutche buggers"

Six of us were in the Gsg9 stores collecting gear for the live training op in St Petersburg, where there were two large kit bags full of stuff already prepped and waiting for us. Most of the kit we had never seen before right down to this piece of apparatus that resembled a headpiece worn by a Star Wars Stormtrooper that was to be known as night sight bobbin, and not to be used for looking at women to see what underwear they have on, a sort of x-ray specs sort of glasses affair contraption.

There was less interesting equipment supplied as well, such as ration packs with corned beef in and shovels and spades, maps and compasses and a new prototype satellite navigation system that Taff wanted to know how to operate.

"Where's the idiots guide to this piece of shit whealtrim"

"Oh, you mean you are looking for the welsh instruction booklet, the one that tells you to turn it on and follow on screen instructions"

"Whealtrim you smartarse"

"Better than being a dumbass, Dumbass. Here, try that lightweight scrim vest on and stop being a woman"!

I threw vented webbed vest towards the large muscle bound and finely tuned frame of Taff who quickly tossed it over his head and studded it up then filled the pockets with as many Heck magazines as possible, in an attempt to create a lean mean killing machine. He picked up one of the large Bowie style hunting knives in the kit, grabbed me by the collar, pulled me towards him and in a deep operatic type voice,

"I like you Whealtrim, that's why I'm going to kill you last"

A roar of laughter filled and echoed around the store room, even the store man was in a temporary state of malfunction, unbeknown to us the store man regularly had momentary mutational misfits of approximately two minutes, which could be brought on even by the slightest bit of humour, somebody hiccupping perhaps or just dropping their pen on the floor after signing on the dotted line of the Gsg9 store requisition order. Imagine this man out with us on a Friday night; we would have to bring a straightjacket out with us.
Connal and Jock picked up their kit back and carried them towards the door, interrupted by the inane store man,

"Wrong door my friend"

He pointed to the other double door which was through a galley way and to the left, Taff, myself and the two Germans followed.

The door opened and led to a large workshop garage in which two Range Rovers were parked next to each other and to the left was a large rectangular table with one chair at either end. In the middle was Major Forrester.

"Good afternoon chaps come around the table if you don't mind.

"Right, four targets to observe in this training operation, so look in at these pictures here, the Kolorov brothers are up to no good, not sure what yet but as a training and observation exercise only, you six have been tasked to find out what they are up to.

You will take residence in a safe house in the suburbs of St Petersburg and take photographs and take note of what these four are up to, follow them in a hire car but on no account get noticed.

It is imperative that they do not know that agencies are watching them. There are six boxes of camera equipment to use, endless amounts of notepads, and so no excuses to not write times down of what they do and where they go.

You will be on location for three weeks and I am told it is minus thirty degrees so in your kit there are heated gel packs to use for outdoor ops, Michael and Stefan here will be your advisors for the duration.

There is a slush fund in the Range Rover to be used for expenses and the like; I have meetings at the home office with the foreign secretary so I will see you in four weeks' time. By the way, this and all future ops are to be deemed as covert so no chin-wagging to absolutely anyone. Last of all, the maintenance staff wanted me to thank you for unseizing the top of the hot water urn; they have been trying to clean it out for years, toodle pip".

"No bloody wonder that brew tasted shite, Taff"

"Ken, it give me the kitchen tiles Mon" (Piles)

"Jock, I'm not sure what's worse, listening to you trying to talk rhyming slang, or listening to you talk about the condition of your arse, shall we get the stuff in the cars and bog off then"

Stefan and Michael were busy counting the slush fund with smiling faces; the last time I had seen a German smile like that was when Boris Becker won at Wimbledon. They had found two thousand pounds sterling, ten thousand German marks and were counting some other money which looked like what you would buy Old Kent road with in that board game you play with your dad till the early hours in the morning.
Michael said it was a little more than last time but there was an extra person and it all got spent on bits and bats, takeaway's etc.

"Ay Connal, what was that deutche blonde like then "?

"Ah she was wicked, she wasn't actually German, she was British but living with a German friend whilst studying at Bonn university. Very intelligent and funny as well,"

"Was she from Essex"?

"No Taff, she was not from Essex, there's me trying to be smart by asking her how she likes her eggs in the morning, and she said in reply as quick as you like, unfertilized thanks!   I couldn't believe it, a wise arse blond bint".

The journey across Germany, north east to St Petersburg was pretty fast, we seemed to cover a lot of miles in a short space of time, two hour stints at the wheel, Michael the German in one car and Stefan the other German in the other, so we could speak in German and practice what to say to potential partners on our social evenings, for instance, "whilst du mit mir bed gehen", that sort of thing.

"Er Michael, this route plan says we are to drive to Berlin and then dump the Range Rovers at a German military base and then fly in a military helicopter up to St Petersburg, does that sound right"?

"Ya mein friend,   that sounds correct"

"Shit, what about customs and borders an all that shit"?

"There are no borders for you now. You can go anywhere and do anything, well almost anything;   you are classed as a diplomat"!

The purring of the Range rover sent me half to sleep which left Michael the German who was driving, and Taff to keep him awake, I could just about hear the brave German ask Taff what a woolyback was.

An hour later we pulled in behind the other car at a service station just outside Gottingen, looked like we were filling up our bellies and the cars here as there was a decent enough looking café alongside the petrol station. Taff filled one and Connall the other,

"Is it full Conall "?

"Ay it's harry toppers pal"

"It's what"?

"Harry toppers, full to the brim, can't get any more in, comprehende "?

"Bloody ell, first of all its Jock and Ken, now we've got a Paddy and a Harry, have you just invented that or summat"?

"No its green lid speak you see"! (Royal Marine language)

"Ah I see, well I'll have to invent one of my own then won't I. Let's park up and get some scram in, bloody Edward starving I am. What about you Michael, Sie ist hunger ya, essen jezt"?

"Your German is getting no better"

"Dumkopf, is that better"?

ST PETERSBURG

The Kolorovs were busy getting drunk in one of their haunts in St Petersburg causing a lot of noise and generally being drunk and disorderly, no one said a thing to them as they owned the club or tea room /café as the name described it on the front of the property.

It was situated in the town centre but away from the commercial buildings and behind a small church. Rumour had it that there were several recent unmarked graves in the church grounds filled with people who had tried to oppose the Kolorovs, some with sliced abdomens and other with cheese wired necks. Nice.

A meeting was about to take place in the café and the biggest of the Kolorov brothers, who was about eight feet tall waved his arm to all the drunken customers and other associates to get out of the area and out of earshot. An accumulation of tables were abstractly placed in the café, but the giant managed to squash them all together with three or four arm movements that the royal philharmonic orchestra conductor would be proud of, one big rectangular sit down. The Ruskies of the square table were about to plan the next villainous outing.

A selection of bottles, vodka, tequila, and more vodka, were placed on the table along with numerous shot glasses, no frills, just men and alcohol.

"You have the shipment organised Mikael"?

"Ya of course, two crates full of mk14,s and lrm (long range missile) launchers, all packed up in Clingfilm wrapped in bubble wrap and surrounded by 2000 silicon covered cuddly toys for protection".

"Ok, I will ring my brother in England with the shipment details, and you have the customs officer's family address"?

"Ya"

Vodka was passed around to celebrate the movement of arms to the next destination, and a plot was discussed to kidnap the customs officer's families and retain them until the package was released.

K-TEAM CARS.

Berlin was now fifty clicks away and according to Michael the German the airport was ten clicks south of Berlin, so at the speed we were travelling that would be about half an hour away.

I put the travel plug- in kettle on with its cigarette lighter socket, and the power on red light glowed. I rubbed my hands together thinking of the delightful cup of tea that was to come in about ten minute's time. Connal passed a Yorkshire tea bag which had been pilfed from some ration packs back at the GSG9 HQ and we discussed and looked forward to a wicked, long awaited brew which would be appreciated by all.

The mini kettle boiled away whilst I prepped the cup and got the milk ready that we had purchased at the petrol garage shop earlier.

Michael overtook the other Range Rover so that we could wave the cup and the tea bag at the other operatives who were drooling back at us.

Michael spotted a rastplatz and suggested we pull in to have a piss and a cup tea, because there was no toilet on the helicopter.

Michael pulled on the handbrake but left the engine running, I placed the boiling water In the cup and with caution opened the door, got out and walked to the back of the car well gingerly like. Connal opened the rear tailgate door and I placed the precious cup of rosy lea on the boot floor and left it to brew for the required two minutes while I found the spoon and tapped it on my hand and hummed a satisfying song of joy.

The other three walked over having parked their Range Rover in front of ours, both vehicles were on a slight incline, but the tea was level.

"Have you got a cup of tea there Boyo"?

"Eye Taff, just about enough for a mouthful each"

All six of us gathered around the tailgate like it was a naffi serving hatch and the boys waited in anticipation for me to put the spoon in and stir thirty two times clockwise and twice anti clockwise. I picked up the spoon, conscious of the glaring eyes and was just about to place it in the cup.

"What's that noise boys "?

I could hear a rolling, rumbling noise coming from the front of the car. I put my head to the side of the boot and saw the other Range Rover rolling backwards in an unstoppable reverse motion, Bang!

"Shit, bloody tea everywhere, bastard! "

Steaming hot tea dripped onto the floor through the slightly discoloured and rusty lower tailgate hinge. Taff in his wisdom attempted a rescue plan in double time. He picked up the toppled empty cup and reached under the tailgate and placed the cup under the drips, managing to collect several mouthfuls of amber nectar. Taff stood up and held the salvaged remnants in front of him and gave a grin of glee and deep joy. What nobody had noticed was the jolt of the vehicles had forced the age weakened hydraulic rams to slowly lower the upper tailgate door and Taff was standing directly under it. The door hit Taff's head, not hard enough to put him down, but enough to shock him into dropping the rescued cup. Tea everywhere again!

"Ken, there's no tea left ya dozy welsh twat"

I walked to the front of the cars and assessed the damage, looked inside the front vehicle and saw that the hand brake had released itself, or should I say someone had left it off, derr!

All of us were disgruntled, dismayed and disappointed at not having tasted the refreshment that was staring us in the face.   None the less, we got back in the cars and set off back on the autobahn towards Berlin.

Within fifteen minutes the disused airfield was in sight. Taff the Welshman with the sore head spotted it and repeatedly described it as looking like an airfield that hadn't been used in a while.

"Taff your power of deductions are far more superior then the average tortoise, our grid references match this airfield to the Inch, this new sat nav thingy confirms we have reached our destination and not only that, Michael has been here before and remembers that worn out hanger there and the ramp and pit next to it with the broken down Lada on it, still there waiting for someone to fix it or scrap it"

"Oh, is it the right place then"

Taff's replies were that of sarcasm and a wild attempt at humour, Welsh humour!

The two Range Rovers parked up and we all got out had a stretch, looking at the two Germans for the next move.

"Ay up Michael, where is our transport to the next stop lad"

"Wir mussen here stayen, velleicht eine stunde" (Stay here for an hour)

"Taff, do you think you can start up the range rover, plug in the travel kettle and make a brew without spilling it all over the place this time, or shall I ask a responsible person to carry out that task?"

"Shut it Wealtrim, or you will suffer a fate far worse than not having a brew for twenty four hours so you will".

It was just under the said hour that we all heard a whirring thumping noise coming from the direction of the hanger, getting quicker and louder, it sounded like some sort of rota turbine engine, possibly a helicopter.

"Ken, see that monster hovering like a mosquito over yonder"

"Yep, looks pretty much like our transport, what do you reckon Michael?"

The aircraft taxied at about 5 feet off the ground to our location and we were surprised to see Major Forrester sitting next to the pilot. He was smoking a ceegar, wearing a huge Stetson and was clearly enjoying the 'Texan' look which actually suited him very well.

The chopper was an American Huey painted gloss black with some sort of crest displayed on the side with a scythe on it. It looked like it was meant to normally carry someone with a bit more importance than us minors. The aircraft landed twenty feet away from us and out stepped JR Ewing, ducking his head and running towards us.

"Right chaps get the gear out of the landies and get them in the hanger, lock em up and put the key in the exhaust, we need all of the equipment in the back end of this bird, then we can get going to St Petersburg, come on chop chop!"

Six bags of kit were thrown in the back of the Huey by most of us, all except for Taff, who for some reason was sprinting towards the hanger with great haste, looking like he had left something behind, moments later he reappeared with the travel kettle in hand.

Pegging it back, Taff jumped in the back of the Huey and asked the pilot if there was a twelve volt cigarette lighter socket on board to plug into.
The pilot turned around and gave a glare that could floor an elephant and pointed to the seat with the orange button in front of it with a piece of masking tape stuck on a plastic trim above the warning light, which showed the comedy effect wordings, EJECTOR SEAT MALFUNCTION WARNING INDICATOR,

"Look at that boyo, I'm wanting to make a brew but in the process will get catapulted upwards and decapitated, charming isnit"

"Ken, what do you expect from a Frenchman"

The helicopter lifted up to five feet again, and slowly gathered speed, then the tail end lifted up slightly as the collective lever was operated, and the frog pilot pushed forward on the joystick and the engine thrust propelled the aircraft ahead and into the sky

"Right chaps, here are your targets, memorise the faces won't you, pass them around Michael if you don't mind. I'll need those dossiers back tomorrow after the surveillance and operations back up team have seen them. Remember lads this is training only, no contact or getting into trouble, St Petersburg has a reputation for, err, leading visitors astray"

"No problems sir, training only. We get the message" Connal replied with a very mature father like voice, pretending that we would all behave ourselves and keep out of mischief, Yeah right. The aircraft landed and we jumped out, after throwing the kit on the floor.

Major Forrester shouted from the chopper.
"Take the mini bus to the operations house, keys on the sun visor and location details under the passenger front seat"

Michael the German gave a sort of wave come salute, a respectful lift of the arm, the sort a king would give to his knight for winning battles. The Huey took off, taking the Major with it, leaving us to drive ourselves in to the tales of the unexpected.

The drive through was cold and busy. The roads were full of old cars, even Ladas, Moskavitchs and Morris Itals were common as muck here. The houses looked grey and miserable, a bit like back home but colder, a lot colder, try minus 40.

"Taff you've got frozen snot hanging from your nose"

"Ken, it's his brains hanging out from his nostrils not snot"

"Bloody heater isn't working is it boyo, cold it is, so it is, isn't it just "

Michael remembered the street from a previous time and pointed us to park in the alleyway to the side of the house.
The door was opened by an attractive middle aged woman wearing business style attire. Her eyes donned designer glasses, looking pretty damn fit as a butcher's dog.

"Kommen sie in, schnell, schnell es ist sehr kalt drausen," (Come in. it's cold outside).

The attractive woman introduced herself as Carmen and offered us coffee. There was no tea as it was too British, apparently. Carmen pointed over to the surveillance team telling us their names as though we would remember them straight away, and then pointed us to the kettle.

"There ya gan Taff, sort brews out Mon, be sharp about it, we are all Ghandi's flip flop here"

"Oh, should I make the brews then,"

We all looked at Taff with an unanimously outvoted look, so he didn't have much choice.

"Ken, are you making a brew or what?

Carmen showed us heaps of intel on our targets, numerous pictures and recordings of these Russian vagabonds, all up to no good.

She explained that we had been commissioned by the Russian special police to gather information on major criminal activities of the Kolorovs and crew. Carmen also said that we were responsible for the observation points outside the house and the house team were responsible for collating the evidence and sending it to the heads of security, i.e. Captain Black and Major Forrester. They in turn would report to the home secretary with a plan of action if there was time. If time was not available, we would act as necessary to prevent any crime.

A tall fella introduced himself as Karl, the operations manager. He instructed us to prepare a flask and a few snacks as there was a reccy shift to carry out. The shift would last about fourteen hours, six of us would use the van parked in the garage, with two, two man teams on foot and two men permanently in the van as back up and radio control.

"Michael you know this area don't you? Follow and watch them like a hawk, see what they are up to, no contact, purely observation, good practice for you lot."

The van was brand new, rented of course, out of the slush fund pocket money that was apparently seized from previous exploits, drug raids and the like. Apparently there was also a collection of cars we had yet to see, and had a value in the millions. Ill-gotten gains, repossessed from the druggies in and around the European scanning area of GSG9. Michael the German had volunteered on two journeys of one hundred and fifty kilometres each way to drive back two of the Daytona yellow lambos, just for experience of course.

The seats in the back of the Mercedes van were more like bar stools screwed on to the floor, no space for seat belts or armrests, and just about enough room to say you weren't in a British rail train. The rest of the back of the van was littered with comms equipment and a steel cupboard which was locked. Michael saw me staring at the mysterious locker with interest and piped up.

"Das ist machinen pistol locker"

Jock overheard Michael and blurted out his usual inquisitive statement.

"Ken I thought there was to be no weapons on this outing, what have we got in there then, a Winchester, Gatling gun or summat more prehistoric."

"Two hecklers, an AK47 and a how do you say a jolly old SLR with scope, Pussers issue with wooden stock and body"

"Wicked, I'll look forward to cleaning that later when we are bored "

Taff was in the front with the map telling the driver the correct way to get to the destination, the one that the driver knew off by heart but Taff had decided that was the longest most awkward route and had reduced the time of travel by half or so he reckoned.

"You see it's all in the contours boyo, follow the contours and you won't go wrong you see. Contours yes that's it boyo, follow them".

The potholes in the road reminded me of the journey from Lancashire to Aldershot on the train with the huge man sat beside me taking up five spaces more than he should, and feeling every bump on the track, every bolt that held the tracks together seemed to be loose, or the track were laid on sleeping policemen or maybe it just wasn't a rolls Royce.
There were no windows in the back of the van so we had to rely on listening to Taff and his running commentary on each left and right turn and oh mind that pothole after the driver had already failed to see it.
 Twenty minutes later we were parked up in what we were told was a cemetery car park which conveniently was two hundred metres from a pub/café bar where there might be some action, as in food and drink.

"Michael might we be able to get some pizza's or summat, I'm starving"?

"No problem, we will all go into the restaurant and have a sit down meal, nobody has a takeaway around here, and if we went in two's people would think we were gay and it would be not right, so we can be on a stag do or similar Yes ?"

"Top banana"

Connal wasn't a man of many words but when he did speak he used the minimal amount of words possible with maximum descriptive impact which usually summed up the situation and mood to a tee.

The restaurant if you can call it that, more like a pole dancing strip club, was an old style flag floored, coal fired, oak beamed, three houses knocked into one type of club, which served food, and ale by the bucket. Why do we not get this at home we all thought and looked at each other and nodded in approval and appreciation of the scantily clad wenches we were surrounded by.

Naturally Michael looked around constantly like a spy, looking for any faces that we needed to be aware of, and during his three sixty degrees scope of the place his face dropped slightly at one corner and his left eye closed in disapproval of what he saw. He took great care not to be noticed by us or the face he had seen, and very quickly put his hand up to try and catch the eye of one of the waitresses to order drinks, but I knew he had seen something or someone and I nodded to him that I knew. He lifted his other hand up with two fingers protruding from it indicating wait two minutes and I will explain.

"Wheels, that bloke over there is one of Kolorov's henchmen, looks like he's having some scran with his girlfriend, maybe we can follow after, quick eat up your pizza rapid style just in case"

Connal barked out the order like he knew all along that the man was there, just neglected to inform us of the fact until he had finished his food, charming!

Two hours later we were still sat at the table, but now had severe indigestion and were extremely rat-arsed having ordered several miles of beer just so we could letch at the legs on show and had almost forgotten about the task in hand. When the man stood up from his seat and projected himself about eight feet upwards, he must have been the tallest man I have ever seen, and looked as though he worked out regularly as his biceps were huge.

His partner had red hair and must have been half his height, she had a small scar on her right cheek next to her jaw line and looked as though someone had tried to put a knife in her mouth and missed.

Whilst I was inconspicuously watching the pair, the others were downing their beers and had already drawn matches as there were no straws and conveniently passed me the smallest match.

"Ken, you've drawn the short one there pal, looks like it's you, get your money out then, and let's get on".

"Bloody ell how much will it be? I don't think I've got a right lot of money on me."

"Put it on your credit card dumb-arse"

"I haven't got one have I; left it at home do you see"

"Stop farting about and pay up, we are going to lose the target, you can stay and wash up if you like? We'll leave you to it,"

Michael couldn't stop himself from laughing and told me that they were winding me up; the bill had already been paid and stressed that we need to get out quick and sort ourselves out, who's doing what.

It ended up that Taff and I would follow the Bigfoot and his girlfriend with Connal and Michael in close support and Jock and the other German would go back to the van and await our instructions.

"Here Taff, do you reckon they are a proper couple like man/woman sort of thing, little and large there, or maybe dad and daughter or summat,

"She does look a bit young for that old bald headed twat!"

We proceeded to follow the pair into the next few alleys and past a few more pubs, but held back and watched them go into a huge prominent Grande looking hotel with a large glass frontage allowing sight of the whole foyer, tables, bars and the concierges desk all in full view.

"Do you reckon they are there for the night Taff"?
"C'mon, let's go and have a drink in the front bit there and see".

Several hours later Jock and Connal appeared, walking through the glass doors and spotted us within seconds.
"You cunts, we've been looking all over for you, what ya doing here?"
Pissed as farts and happy as Larry, we looked at them with our where have you been all night hurry up and get to the bar expression.

"We are observing the (hiccup) target of course, what else "

"Well for your very intelligent information Dickhead, the target walked out the back kitchen door of the hotel about two hours ago, he must have realised that he was being watched! We have now got to wait here for Michael the German to return with our new orders."
"Get the beers in then and stop moaning you woman"

"Ok"

Michael the German told us the next morning that the night didn't go very well and we weren't to drink as much the next time, however movements of several key figures were noted if not by us then by the rest of the crew. Things were happening and the next exercise was a night op on a warehouse in the middle of a forest, so no beer.

THE CONSALLO HOUSEHOLD

The Consallo family were having dinner in the sitting room of the farmhouse admiring the Italian red wine and looking over the stables where the daughters' horse was kept. Michael was still puzzled and bothered over the bidding system at the council and the odd events surrounding his bid, but still managed a smile towards his adoring daughters face.

"What's wrong Papa "?

"It's nothing, just a deal at work not going to plan, not yet anyway. It will though, no problem, I'll make another offer. "

Although this answer didn't really satisfy daughter Alana, she nodded in polite approval not really knowing if the deal would go any better at all, but she kept out of all family business as she was considered too young to worry herself and would be told to carry on and be a teenager and have fun.

"Papa I met a new friend at school today, she is in the same class as me. She is Irish, just moved over from Northern Ireland with just her mum; her Dad is in the Army. She is nice, can I bring her to see my horse."

"Of course dear, I might not be in but you will be ok won't you?"

"You are working on a Saturday Papa?"

"Yes, I have to try and find out why a stretch of land is very important to other people, that's all."

Michael's investigators were trying their best to find out who wanted the docklands deal, who else would be that keen to build houses and have the available money?
One of the investigators was sitting in his car observing the land through a pair of binoculars from a high point and could see a team of about six men with a big drill on a tripod, two of the men had pens and clipboards and appeared to be writing information down and putting samples into containers. This had been going on for at

least four hours, a team of scientists maybe taking samples or maybe just looking for treasure.

The investigator stayed for another half hour observing and then thought of a plan to get some information. If he were to walk over to the team of diggers and ask if they had seen a dog, maybe he could have a nosey at what they were doing and perhaps even ask them what they were up to.

It took the investigator about fifteen minutes to actually get within talking distance of the group, he knew they had spotted him and were fiddling about with something in one of the small rucksacks they had on the floor next to their feet amongst the grass and heather.

"Excuse me; don't suppose you have seen a black Labrador have you? He was running up towards this area; I think he saw a rabbit or something"

"No."
"Are you sure? I'm sure he came this way."
"No!"

The answer was spoken abruptly and the men clearly didn't want to engage in conversation, but he thought he would give it one last friendly try.

"What are you doing here, research or something?"

One of the men came close and spoke in a punctuated, threatening tone.

"Private, confidential, research."

"Leave you to it then", the investigator said, as he walked away pleased with the outcome of his decision. Clearly something strange was going on.

THE BOYS

"Taff, you got my thermal socks have you"?

"Well it's like this isnit boyo, when I borrowed them, I had them for three and a half days and they began to smell a bit so what I did was I washed them then didn't I, then I put them on again wet so as to help wear my new boots in, which were also wet me having soaked them in the bath for a few hours, the result of which was a perfectly fitting well worn in pair of pussers Para boots"

"Is that a yes or a no to my perfectly acceptable question Taff"?
"It's a no, because what happened was, the boot softening mission was such a success that Connal wanted to do the same with his boots and hence forth used the same socks but when they started to smell he washed them in diluted bleach mixture, which wasn't diluted to the correct formula so the end result was a pair of socks which resembled a woman's woolly scarf with more than a few holes in, and I'm not entirely sure what happened to them after that".

"Taff shut the fuck up and make a brew"

Michael the German was being briefed by Captain Black on what the next mission was, although can't really see why a bit of a reccy outing needed this much attention, just a simple few holes in a field with a couple of pairs of binos, what more fuss do you need!

"Taff have you got those grids right, it can't be here, we are under a canal bridge and supposed to be digging a hush hush pit to spy in "

"I have got them dead right I have"

"Taff, it's pitch black and you want me to dig you an observation trench through a concrete surface with a pussers spade which resembles a big spoon, well I know I'm up for most things but this takes the Captain Jenkins (biscuit, so called as in basic training custard creams etc)"

"Well it's just to the right isnit boyo over there where there is plenty of grass and loose soil, I can smell it don't you see, I can, I was brought up in this shit, wasn't I just".

Michael the German pointed over to the same place as Taff had pointed to and duly noted that this area has been used before as an observation post and overlooks the disused tinned food factory over in the crook to the left of the grassy knoll.

Michael dumped a supplies bag, which also had equipment in it, including two more digging spoons and some tins of corned beef.
Jock, Connal and the German were observing elsewhere, in fact somewhere a lot warmer as in a Range Rover, parked up at the nearest tourist spot. In fact, nowhere near us, only just enough distance away to still have contact through the walkie talkies.

Ken, there's no heater in this heap of British shite man, have ya geet a blanket Mon? "
"Eye, there's a pussers woolly g10 issue one here pal. "

Before Connal could finish his sentence Jock let out a cry of elation.

"Thank Christ for that man, I'm freezing my knackers off here!"

"Underneath this ant's nest in the corner of the truck "
"Oh shite you are jesting me "

"Nope, you have a choice of ants in the right side of the car, or on the other side, spiders and mould"
"Oh the agony of choice, I'll ponder on it for a wee while so I will."

An hour and a half passed and the three were struggling to get to sleep in the car with no heater.
The cold silence was interrupted by a crackle on the comms,

"Bravo two Zero radio check over"

"Ken just ignore him, the prick! They are probably warmer than us, the wankers"

"Bravo two Zero radio check over"

"He's probably just piss balling about Mon, let him carry on for a wee bit, make him think he is on own"
"Bravo two Zero come in, radio check. Over"

Jock eventually picked up the mike and pressed the transmission button

"What do ya want wheeltrim"

"Bravo Two Zero in position and target in sight along with four other targets"

Michael the German being the experienced observer in command pricked his ears up and almost snatched the receiver off Jock

"Wheels, who else ist mit the target,"

"Two big geezers in a small van and a woman and man in another car, looks like they are yapping to each other about summat"

"Wheels maintain radio silence until we get there"

Taff could hear a rustling of branches coming from behind us indicating that the rest of the boys were here already, or that a herd of meerkats were descending upon us.

"Taff is that them?"

"All I can see is three figures wearing black camouflage gear coming towards us at a great rate of knots, bloody noisy twats they are, broken more twigs in coming here than a Lumberjack walking to work"

Michael lifted up the leaf, branch and local foliage decorated Hessian cover which was hiding our pit and jumped in to borrow the bino's

"Sheisse, man!! It's all of them all in one place Sheisse!!

"What's up me old boxhead friend "?

"See that woman there, she is what you might call a general or commandant of the operation and those two dumbkopfs sat in the van are the main henchmen of the operation, they are very dangerous men, they always stick together making them a force to be reckoned with, they are both about eight feet tall and nine feet wide, Sheisse "!

"What's the problem Michael? We are only on a reccy, we could keep stum and just observe!"

"You don't understand, if they are all here something is going down. I have to get word to Carmen at HQ. Okay, stay here and only move backwards, watch what they do, absolutely no contact whatsoever, you don't have weapons to cope with these people"

"Ok, Chill"

Michael retreated the same way he came in but making even more noise than before. We heard the car wheel spin off back to base.

"Ken what's up with Lurch the noo, he seems to be away with the fairies Mon"

Jock didn't hear the conversation I just had with Michael and being the inquisitive sort thought he'd want to know what had occurred.

"Well it is like this ya see, he said we have to get a wee bit closer to the target, observe sort of closer like and see what mischief we can cause to disrupt their grand plan."

"Ah, I see the grand plan ploy!"

"Connal, what ya looking for pal"

"Bloody bino's have done a runner can't see a piggin thing in this shithole"
"That's because I've hidden them in my woolly hat, so as not to drop them in any cow shit, Again!

We all put stealth mode in place and crawled our way to the building quiet and invisible like.
 The voices were getting louder now and the Russian speak was more difficult to understand, one of the sasquatch henchmen tossed the remnants of his cigarette towards our direction, about ten foot away, and the embers sparked a tiny fire in the bracken, lighting up a circular area to which almost shed a glow on our position. He cursed some obscenities, then lit up another and continued with the pow wow.

We had to wait crouched down for a further twelve point two minutes before the group of villains moved into the building out of the cold.

Connal slowly lifted himself up and did a three sixty with his eyes, then made a signal with his fist and moving fingers to motion us forward and split into two groups and cover the sides of the building. The two fingers pointed in front of Connal's eyes was not a disgusting hand gesture, it was a sign to watch and observe for lookouts coming back out of the building and spotting us.

The small windows in the building were fairly high up and required a leg up which was left to Connal and Jock. Taff the sheep and I slowly sneaked around the building watching what we were walking on as there were several shards and shrapnel of some sort of small explosion scattered about the loosely concreted floor surface surrounding the building.

Every step created a crunch under our feet which fortunately were only heard by passing rats and insects.

We passed two doors which appeared disused, slightly broken around the hinge area, like someone had tried to kick off its hinges. We approached the back of the building where two more vans were parked, reversed up to a ramp with the rear doors fully open ready to load something or someone in the back. I looked at Taff inquisitively to which he shrugged his shoulders and pointed to the small shed in front of the vans, suggesting that we made our way there for a better viewpoint inside the building.

Taff was the first to crouch down behind the shed and signalled me to move from my current position whilst he covered and watched. Green fluorescent lights shone through from inside the building emitting rays of light through the cracks and holes in the doors we had passed earlier, with interrupted patterns from people walking inside the rooms of the building, and smoke signals rose from thrown cigarette butts in a corner of the room.

The view was still fairly limited but several people were talking and seemed to be giving instructions to each other.

I whispered to Taff a question of what to do. I guess the answer "I'm starving" meant he didn't hear what I said! I looked at him again, but instead of asking the same question again I nudged him and pointed to the man walking outside the building and towards the building we were hiding behind. What was odd was that both of his hands were caressing his stomach in a roundward motion, indicating something wrong had passed through his abdomen and was inflicting discomfort.

The door to the shed opened, we heard a clicking noise like a belt buckle unclipping and a slight thud as though something heavy but not solid had dropped on the floor.

Seconds later, a disgustingly rancid seven second rasping fart noise projected from within, echoing and almost vibrating the thin wood tongue and groove constructed shed, followed by a sigh of relief and another short burst of gas.

Taff looked at me repulsed, his face turned and twisted unnervingly, his moustache stood on end like a cat's tail sensing danger, and then the toilet flushed and Taff managed to force the words

"Shite that was disgusting boyo"

The door opened and the big Rusky walked out rebuckling his belt whilst increasing pace muttering some more obscenities and lighting a cigarette.

We could see Connal and Jock both doing sneaky beaky walk around the back of the building but they did not have a good view inside like us. Taff tried to distract them with abstract hand signals. Taff said earlier that he had studied semaphore at the library in Harlech where he lives, so he must presume that everybody else understands him.

Connal saw Taff waving at him and slowly walked towards us, but not passing the gable end of the building, Jock followed. BANG, CLATTER, TING BANG, breaking the night silence, the noise of an old rusty steel bin lid falling of the top of a two foot high coal bunker, filled the misty air. Jock didn't see the perfectly placed and angled sweeping brush that was holding the lid upright against the wall.

"Fucking twat man" Jock cursed, as he sprinted for cover.

The racket brought all the people from inside rushing out, guns in hand raised and pointed in the direction of the noise. Jock and Connal had pegged it and were long gone. The Russian boss woman pressed down on one of the henchman's assault rifles forcing it to the floor, shouted to him, "Alive Alive", and pointed to each corner of the area surrounding the building.

"Come on let's do one Taff", I signalled to him, while I still thought we had a chance of getting away, but two men running on loose gravel just can't be silent.

We could hear boots on the ground behind us gathering speed and closing the gap. We must be able to beat these characters, they are dressed in completely the wrong gear for running, not us, we had lightweight combat pants and smocks, and we should cuff these mothers!

Taff was ahead of me when I saw him crouch down and pick up a stick whilst running, maybe some sort of weapon; I would have to do the same. The seven foot lurch chasing after me was gaining even more ground so I didn't have the chance nor did I see any sticks the right size. Thoughts raced through my mind,

'Shall I slow down and all of a sudden bend over sideways and let the Rusky fall over my arched back. Hopefully he will end up on the deck. Taff would race back to the rescue with his stick and beat the hell out of him. Not sure if that would work he looks about seven feet tall and five feet wide, he would probably take me with him, and I would get squashed'.

I ran a little more and thought a little more, but it was too late. The Rusky flew at me with a perfect rugby tackle, arms around my waist, locking his hands at the front, and allowing his arms to slide down the lower half of my body forcing my legs to stop moving. I tried desperately to twist my falling body so as not to land on my face. Crunch; My right shoulder hit the floor first and then my neck, followed by excruciating pain from ear to ear. 'Shit I've landed in a bed of nettles', I thought. I lifted my neck upwards to escape the offending plant and to see if I could throw a punch. Too late, Bam, a fist the size of a fully grown tortoise planted itself right on my chin, just next to my Kirk Douglas dimple. Shit, the pain felt horrible, the Rusky was still grabbing my legs and going for another punch.

I reached behind me scraping the grass with my palm facing upwards, fingers open, forcing it into several nettle plant stems, just underneath the nettle leaf so as not to sting myself, and gathered in my palm several crispy stinging nettle leaves. I thrust the vegetational weapon directly into his dull set eyes and scrunched, twisted and rubbed in the green.

It took a second to work but the reaction was perfect. Both of his hands were forced to touch and feel the wound and try and make it better, but the rubbing just made it worse inflicting more pain and misery on the Russian.

I seized the opportunity and took the biggest swing I could with a karate shot on his nose,   blood spurted everywhere, what a mess. He managed to get up on his knees, hands still protectively covering his face, not really knowing what to do other than attempt to stand up. I realised he was in a position to kick or run at me again, so I wound my arm up around my back and with an open hand did a roundhouse rocket slap right on his ear. I've never seen a person topple over sideways and head first before now. He was out.

Taff appeared by my side.

"Come on Wheeltrim stop fannying around ya divvy!"

We disappeared into the woods making our way back to the RV point, where luckily enough Jock, Connal and Michael the German were all laughing and giggling like school children.

"Ken   what's happened to your mooth, Wheels have ya bin skelped ya wee poof? "

"That ten foot sasquatch Russian twat gave me a fist full didn't he."

"You have just been to dentist yes? "
Michael the German butted in with yet another piss take comment.

Back at the hq house there was cups of coffee waiting for us as we walked in, don't know who made them but I was

[149]

curious so I walked over to the kitchen and picked up the coffee jar, I was right Carmen had made them, and the reason I know this, is that only women put the coffee jar top on cross threaded,   I should have been named Hercule Poirot.

 Good brew anyway, there's something about the way German women make brews, very European, very tasty, very milky.

Michael came in with a new set of instructions from his five minute meeting with Captain Black and Major Forrester, who had both flown in from meetings with some bigwigs.

"Listen boys we have orders, we are to travel to the sea port and get on the same Ferry as the baddies we have just encountered, they have been followed and seen boarding the boat to the tip of Germany, how do you say err Get shit your,   err, yes that's it, get together your shit yetz machen".

"I havni finished ma brew yet ya wee bassa"!

"Intelligence just coming in now chaps, the Kolorovs and their team of villains have been seen in convoy, six vehicles in total heading for the boat, let's be off. Something's happening just not sure where, we have to follow,"

Major Black was reluctant to give us more information but he knew more for definite, why was he coming with us, why had he prepared several hard backed alloy suitcases, one with a hazardous chem badge on it. Why was he wearing combats?

CONSALLO HOUSEHOLD

Michael Consallo was deep in conversation with the boss of his team of investigators discussing what have they found out about the land. He was informed that sample pile diggers had been there for a few weeks.

"Michael, we have already been through the council deeds and history of the land and apart from a suspected unconfirmed minimum amount of some minerals sunk about one hundred feet below the surface, there is nothing."
"Hmmm, I don't believe there is nothing, what sort of minerals?"
"Err I have it written down here in my notebook, Polyhalite"
"What is that used as, or for?"
"Not sure Michael, in laboratories I guess"
"Well find out, what am I paying you for Marone!!!"

Michael walked off back to the house muttering to himself. Polyhalite sounds like bomb making stuff, what on earth would they want with Polyhalite? He thought about who he might know that had access to a lab or a chemist or physician. Nobody came to mind except his policeman crime scene friend who he had not spoken to since encouraging him to bet on one of his horses.

Michael had described it as a sure thing at the time, unfortunately the horse lost and subsequently his friend lost a large amount of money and they had not spoken since. Michael couldn't think of anybody else who could help him so he took a diamond cut brandy glass from the rosewood drinks cabinet in the drawing room of his farmhouse mansion, and half filled it with Courvoisier, expecting the liquid to install several tons of confidence in the call he now had to make

"Ah   Steven Moss my old friend, how are you and your family?"
"Who is this? Oh is it the best tipster in the UK, the one that looks after his mates when the chips are down and they need a win, yes I thought it was you,   got any more tips???"
"Are you still sore about that race? What are a few dimes against friends? The horse fell what could I do?"
Steven knew Michael wanted something when he asked how his family were, but it must have been important for him to pick up the phone. Steven considered it may be opportunity to recover the two thousand pounds he lost so softened his tone.
"How are you and your family Michael? What can I do for you?"

"It's a long story Steven, but are you still in the CSI labs?"

"Yeah but only part time, I spend some time out in the field now, why what's up?"

"I could do with knowing what Polyhalite is used for"

"Polyhalite, what on earth do you need that for?"

"I don't need it; I just want to know what it is"

"It's a mineral that has four nutrients in it, potassium, sulphur, magnesium and calcium, normally used in the commercial production of agricultural fertilizer. So, are you thinking of getting into plant food then Michael"?

"No, something completely and utterly nothing to do with plant food. I'm trying to buy some land to build houses on which might have polyhalite content somewhere on the plot"

"Very interesting Michael, yes very interesting, can I come and see you with my detective friend"?

"Yes I'm in this afternoon".

Steven arrived at Michael Consallo's house with three detectives including the chief superintendent, all dressed in civvies so as not to arouse any gossip or suspicion. A three hour discussion ensued, with two of the detectives writing notes Steven the lab tech was drinking brandy with Michael as he was off duty and interrupting the POW POW with horse shit talk.

K-Team

The ferry boat to Rostock Germany from St Petersburg was not an option to follow the Kolorov's so an alternative form of transport was arranged.

The black Huey with the Russian garden tool insignia on the side was waiting for us outside a building that looked like a tool shop. The tool shop however, actually contained weapons of mass destruction. There were three steel shelving units along the left wall draped with cloth Hessian taupe, and to the opposite wall were screwed two high up alloy kitchen type cupboards. The taupe was pulled back to reveal four l.a.m's (land to air missile launchers) with huge shells that had a shiny serrated cone shaped tip on each of them. Several hand grenades were slotted next to them with almost perfect uniformity.

Captain Black walked in the room and blatted out a statement to the effect of,

"You don't need to bother with those we won't be needing them today", and proceeded to open the Ikea looking kitchen units on the opposite side of the room.

"This is what you want"

A row of six boxes lay on the first shelf; the Captain picked up four of them, and passed them to Taff.

"Dish them out to the boy's boyo".

Trying to inject a bit of humour whilst giving a command was a skill that Captain Black hadn't quite mastered yet, however if he would have just added the words "You welsh Prick" on the end of the command, the result would have made at least one of us emit a polite laugh for at least half a minute!

We were all given a box containing a browning nine millimetre pistol and told to load the magazine with the rounds supplied and be sure that the safety catches were applied before boarding the Huey.

The now familiar wop wop wop noise of the forty eight foot diameter main rotor propelled us into a steep ascent over the treetops and towards the clouds.

Captain Black removed a file from his brief case, Taff tied the lace on his Para boot correctly in a double bow, and Connal was trying to write a letter of some description, Michael the German and Jock were arguing about football.

I was just taking everything in; wondering when is the best time to mention our salary or lack of it. We hadn't been paid since the time we had to march up to the makeshift pay office, a desk slat in the middle of the parade ground, the evening before our forty eight hour pass. Not that we needed anything or had the time to spend anything, we had all that slush money that we saw Michael take charge of, that's a point.

"Here Michael, don't suppose you know what the pay order is here do you?   Do we actually get paid, or is it gratis everything and spend all that money you have in your sky rocket"?

"Sky rocket, what is sky Rocket?"

"Well sky rocket is normally something pointed with some sort of propellant attached to help it jettison into space, however on this occasion it has another meaning, and that is in the form of Cockney rhyming slang in relation to pocket, which is that piece of cotton sewn on to your trouser arse".

"Ah so, Ich verstehen sie", *I understand) ya well, we get a salary which is a bit how you say, Shite! But as you said earlier, all things we need here are paid for by the money we have in the pot, and the money we seize in all of our raids, and there have been a few. This includes the possession of expensive cars which get sold at an auction and the proceeds go in the pot, also there are houses which have been sold and boats, if you need anything, Pizza's or socks or a woman for the night   just ask and I will arrange money for you"

"Now you mention it I could do with a new toothbrush, any chance?

"Naturlich, I also will say to the Major to give you the bank details of your account which is in Switzerland. You also have Diplomatic status, and an ID card to prove it, so this means you have access to tax free just about everything"

"Oh Yeah forgot about that piece of card in my wallet, bit like a passport I suppose with a big red capital D in the right corner, can't wait to show that to my policeman mate in the uk, that will piss him right off, "

Jock was trying to butt in on the conversation at the earliest convenient moment without being rude for a change.

"Ken you don't have any mates in the uk ya wee poof "

"What is Poof "? Asked Michael the German

The Captain passed several items of literature to Michael who in turn passed them on to all of us for a concentrated perusal whilst we were admiring the forest below which was approximately fifty feet away from the aluminium skids of the Huey.

The forest followed the autobahn route on either side and resembled a scene from the parting of the seas, just a sea of green, with grey matter in the middle. The pilot increased his speed to put his mind off the added stress of low flying, presuming that had he had a lapse of concentration the extra speed would allow him to evade the danger. At least the extra adrenalin made him more comfortable, a true battle pilot!

Captain Black picked up the sat phone from his briefcase and made a call, his voice was loud but none of us could hear what he was saying, a few head nods and neck scratches later the Captain replaced the phone and informed us all that our targets had changed cars at a rastplatz approximately one hundred and fifty kilometres from our location. We had to stay approximately fifty clics away at all times as there were other agents on the case who were also in cars.

After about an hour we landed for a short pit stop at a small German air force airfield. More fuel was needed just in case we had to fly all the way through Germany, or to infinity and beyond. Michael explained that the targets would almost definitely be travelling south west as this is their normal route to their wrongdoings. Through Germany, heading west to either France or the UK, they very rarely frequented any other destination. A short sharp money making expedition of a criminal order was their weekly routine. We reboarded the helicopter after a ten minute recess in the gentleman's powder room where we had a piss stop, piss take and a pizza from the canteen on camp.

Captain Black tucked himself in a corner put his feet up, closed his eyes. A tired man on a mission.
 Taff regained his rapidly diminishing acting skills and pretended he was Jon   Wayne in a horse mounted pistol shoot out scene whilst affixing his seat belt, legs akimbo straddling the ass, arms in the air one arm swinging a Winchester rifle, the other a pretend leather lasso.

"Taff you Dick, stop waking the Captain up with your inane body functions, you're as mad as a box of frogs, and you'll never make a Marlon Brando!"

"I've met him don't you know, I have boyo. He was making a film in Wales he was, but I can't for the life of remember what the film was called,"

"Was it The Godfather Taff?"

For some reason or other Taff twisted his neck slow style, like a robot, blinked his eyes,   instigating missile lock on my thigh muscle. Wham, a flying dead leg punch from his right hand crunched my left leg, in jest of course, but god did it hurt.
"Oh, good one Taff that was a cracker!"

I watched his neck slowly robotting to the other leg.

"No No No"

I managed to manoeuvre my body away from the Welshman and his tantrum. Connal tried the 'peace be with you break it up girls' routine without success. Jock was the one that managed to calm the copter with the "seems like from nowhere" production of an extra large pewter hipflask, engraved front and back with Black Watch emblems, along with an accompanying cheesy grin across his face.

"Drink chaps?"

The stinging hot taste of light brown Scottish mouthwash was very welcome.

"Wow Jock you're just a Voodoo child, perfect timing me old china"

I passed the flask still very full to Connal who was drooling and asking if it was Irish, to which I answered, "I haven't the slightest but its mega so it can't be." Even the pilot had some.

It was time to land, not only did we all need a piss after supping whisky for the last half hour or so, but there was a phone call on the sat phone to say that it was now necessary to follow our target by car. The Audi's were waiting for us! I didn't know how they got from the GSG9 hq to our pick up point, but who gives a shit, we were going to be driving what had to be the most powerful cars in Germany.

The Huey landed about thirty feet from a fuel station on an Autobahn not far from an unknown at this moment town in West Germany. A team of four men were waiting on the car park to hand over the vehicles and instructions, one of which was to say that we had to catch up to the live tailing vehicle approximately five clicks in front and travelling at one hundred and twenty kilometres an hour. Taff and myself jumped in the front car and Michael the German, Connal and Jock in the other, two way radio systems were turned on, keys turned, ignition fired, wheels were spinning, off we went.

Both cars soon accelerated to one hundred and sixty km an hour in an attempt to relieve the live vehicle. Regardless of the speed it seemed like an age before we could even speak to the forward car. The radio's had a range of about five clicks (kilometres) in good weather and we were still out of range. To complicate matters, a German Polizei patrol car zoomed up behind us lights flashing indicating us to pull over. Taff noticed there was a rastplatz within a safe distance, about two hundred metres, he indicated to pull in early to let the police know we had seen them. The other car with Connal, Michael and Jock had passed us earlier in race games proving they could actually reach the two hundred and thirty km's an hour before we reached the target car, so we were on our own.

Taff turned the engine off and noticed two of the three policemen quickly exited their car and were rushing towards us, but what was more disturbing was the fact that two of them had drawn their weapons and were pointing them at both of us.

"I think we might be in the sticky stuff here boyo, they don't look very happy"

Before I could reply to the obvious my door flung open and a very irate uniform pointed his gun at me and screamed something in German I wasn't really sure of, but the hand movements made me think he wanted me to get out and place my hands on the bonnet of the car so that's what I did, Taff did the same.

"Reisepasse yetz, schnell, schnell" (Passport please, quick, quick)

I moved my arm from the bonnet and reached into my lightweight pocket thinking my wallet was there, it was not, it was where I left it in the helicopter.

"Shit, Taff you got your ID on you? That should keep em happy"

"Wheeltrim you never seem to amaze me, you always seem to have nothing you need at the right moments and everything you don't at the wrong moments"

"Is that a yes or a no then? I just think this policeman is in a rush"

"It's a yes"

Realising we weren't German, the policeman tried to speak to us in English with a calmer tone, but still firm as you like.

"Passport please" adding, "what were you thinking travelling at one hundred and eighty kilometres an hour in a one hundred km an hour limit where in the middle of the roadworks"

"Well it's like this you see, we're are on a mission of importance and require a certain few allowances here and there don't you know boyo"

Taff passed the policeman his ID card and said, "this is my colleague and we are travelling together on important business."

The policeman nearest to Taff took his ID and looked at it with a puzzled face then looked at his two other uniformed friends shaking his head, muttering words of disbelief and unsurety. He passed the card to his other colleague who had now got out of his car to join in on the arrest.

"Ich weis ich night, was ist en das "(What is that I don't know)

"Diplomatisch, Sheisse, es ist eine diplomatisch man Oh got" (Shit Diplomatic man)

"Erm Err many apologies mein herr we must let you go now but please you could speed the road down here thank you and Gute fahrt " (travel well)

Taff and I jumped back into the super car and sped off before, slowing down at one hundred and fifty clicks an hour just in case the plod decided to stop us again. I called on the two way radio to Connal in the other car, Michael the German answered and with an inquisitive tone asked where the fuck had we been.

"Oh and how are you Michael, nice to hear from you again,"

I was genuinely asking about his health, sarcasm had nothing to do with it, honest.

"Just quit with the chit chat and catch up you fanny"

"That German is getting a bit too big for his boxhead boots, the blond haired prick, we'll have to sort him out, give him a regimental bath or summat. Yeah, we can throw him in that lake yonder Taff to the right over there. Are you listening or what"?

Taff looked at me with utter shock and horror, "Wheels, I've had my hand on the transmitter button for the last ten mins!"

"Oh Oh"

Connal spoke this time on the mike,

"Forget all that we are five clicks away from the target stay alert stay alive, let's be careful out there"

CONSALLO HOUSEHOLD

Michael Consallo was sitting down in a lecture room at York University. He had specifically come to listen to this professor giving a lecture on polyhalite, its properties and fusion capabilities, its chemical and mineral imbalances and its abilities to enhance the production of other commercial products. Michael thought the lecture would bore any normal person to tears; however this hour long introduction to the mineral might give him an insight as to why that piece of land was so sought after.

Michael's concentration was intermittently distracted by the slightly more interesting weird and wacky youthful attire of the students in the lecture theatre, amazed by the wide variety of future boffins to be.

Some had John Lennon style rounded glasses; others ginger sideburns and pierced ears, teenage acne still evident. One teenager had a huge forehead that reminded him of the Tefal TV advert. He chuckled to himself recalling the slightly alien look of the Tefal professor.

The lecturer had a very deep vibrato opera tone to his speech, the sort of voice an auctioneer or a prime minister might have. He spoke with authority and knowledge but the monotony of the lecture and Michaels disinterest in the subject did little to aid his understanding or retention of the shared knowledge. Michael had already forgotten the majority of the lecture and checked his watch hoping it would end soon.

Michael Consallo drank another well deserved espresso whilst sat in the aptly named cottage lecture coffee room, even at four pounds fifty per cup he was on his third wake up and go drink. Contemplating the technical information he had just endured he still did not understand to what end the land would be useful for other than building and who on this earth would want this that much that they couldn't acquire the said land legally.

K-Team

"Connal, don't get too close to that god dam target will you, don't want them getting missile lock on us and pointing a sam (surface to air missile launcher) at us, if they have one in that there van of theirs."

"That's right Wheeltrim, wouldn't like that beautiful face of yours damaged would we you ugly sod".

"Shut it Paddy"

Connal eased off the pedal slightly but kept the target van in sight, while trying to prevent being spotted. Not entirely sure if it worked as they kept changing lanes, maybe as a test to see if we copied. We had managed to stay within five hundred metres of the target at most times in the last six hours. The traffic was grim at this time of day to say the least; there were all sorts of vehicles trying to block our view. The usual rush hour cars and trucks plus the wannabe rally drivers in their BMW's thinking they had the edge over us in our road beast. Overtaking us to prove a point that they thought they had more power, and slowing again to goad us into a race. Unbeknown to them our motor was a performance tuned v-eight four point seven litre engine with approximately five hundred and twenty horses powering it. Not a force to be reckoned with and the temptation to demonstrate was hard to resist, but resist we must!

We had passed signs for every town you can think of in Germany, passing all the main cities, even saw signs for France. These Ruskies were heading for a ferry port; it was just a question of which one? Ostend, Calais or Cherbourg perhaps, and then what? There would be trouble ahead somewhere someplace and we would stop it. We were after all on a recce training operation only, no contact whatsoever.

The car boots were full of special tools for the times when they might be needed. This included "flash bang explosives, machine pistols I haven't seen before, sledge hammers?? Why would we have sledge hammers? Two way radio blocking equipment, gps comms equipment, black one piece overalls with gas masks and night vision glasses, four Browning G10 issue pussers pistols with extended magazines, one mini missile launcher, eight pairs of various sized German Para boots, two packets (100 each) large tie wraps, two small begins, one packet extra-large nappies, not entirely sure why we had those yet, and one complete first aid kit. All this recce equipment made me wonder what we would bring with us for a non recce full contact operation!

Michael the German indicated and decelerated the Audi into the rastplatz and we followed.

"I need piss"

"Oh thanks for that Michael. Taff you may as well get the coffees in ya wee poof, "

Jock had a particular way of delivering a direct order without it sounding like an order and being a total piss take at the same time as giving an insult which wasn't offensive, which we all grew to love and adore. Not.

Walking back from the rastplatz cafe strutting our stuff heading towards the Audi's, Taff noticed that one of the cars looked a little down on one side.

"I think the car has a flat tyre hasn't it by Jove so it has "

"What's that Taff me old fruit? "

"That tyre looks flat at the bottom doesn't it?"

"No shit Sherlock, do ya think it might have a puncture Taff"?

Taff spent a minute looking at the said flat bottomed tyre.

"Well it might have a puncture but I don't think that is the reason why it has gone flat".
"Oh you don't do you.   Prey Taff, what other possible reason would a perfectly serviceable previously fully inflated tyre have for being flat just at the bottom then wisearse Welshman"

Taff reached down towards the tyre and picked out of the valve a small piece of wood that had the remnants of a phosphorous red tip on it. With a full forward leg movement and matching arm swing to boot, the actors stance striked a pose once more

"Yes it's the old matchstick in the tyre valve ploy, oldest boy play in the book, I used to do that to the local policeman's car when he parked outside the station back in the village I did"

"Taff stop prancing about like a Jessie and get the air inflator out of the boot you nob"

"I was just emphasising the fact that when I was little I used to play games on the locals in the village like tying string to all the door knobs on the doors of the terraced houses on the street, then pulling the string and doing a runner, when all the people came out altogether wondering who was knocking on their doors, then the policeman couldn't drive after me as well because he had a flat tyre because I had put a matchstick in his tyre valve, which let his air out and was just like this one here as it happens so it was, wasn't it just!"

"Taff as much as we would all like to listen to you reminiscing about your tales of your youth and "knock a door run" antics, we have a much more pressing item of importance to consider, which is the fact of blowing this flat bottomed tyre up and the tool for the said job is knackered, so any idea's from your knowledge of good ideas, Smartarse?"

"Well what you do is, you go ask that man over yonder at the recovery breakdown depot to borrow his foot pump that's what you do isn't it boyo"

"Back in a tic"

Connal proceeded to walk over to the autobahn werkstat to try out his newly learnt German speak. As lazy and as Irish as Connal was, he was definitely not shy and was up for anything! That said he was reckoning to come back with at least a foot pump.

Michael the German, Taff, Jock and I waited for five minutes, then watched in pure shock as Connal pointed over to us whilst talking to this tall blonde Dolph Lundgren look alike complete with matching flattop hair piece and bulging biceps the size of Bournemouth pier.

Both men climbed into a bright yellow Day-Glo coloured hgv recovery vehicle that had what appeared to be some sort of hydraulic boom mounted to the rear.

A huge cloud of smoke puffed its way out of the exhaust as it started up, and then the driver jerked the clutch from its biting point forcing the vehicle into forward motion, Dolph manipulated the huge steering wheel in rotational left and right movements directing the monster towards us, the quick shift sixteen speed gear box sounded a whistle in-between changes denoting an air assisted movement. It had an American style grill and fender to the front with multiple lights to add to its authenticity of being a huge and gross looking American overweight and overpriced and over in Germany recovery truck.

Connal opened the yellow door of the monster and jumped what seemed to be ten feet, it was high enough to make him land on two feet and bend his knees.

"I've got us a compressor to blow up yon flat bottomed tyre fellas, vielen Danke Mein Herr,"

Dolph stepped out of the truck; he was so tall he didn't have to jump, engaging the PTO switch on his way out. He unlocked a side bin to the driver's side of the vehicle and removed and unravelled a black oil saturated air line with a tyre inflator valve attached to it. He walked over to the flat bottomed tyre, trailing the pipe on his right side dragging leaves, twigs and other articles of nature with it. The corner of the Audi raised itself level to the rest of the car as the air passed through the valve and into the tubeless moulded rubber.

Michael the German talked to Dolph for a while in undescriptive German which we were sure contained words that we should hear, however they were laughing with one another so all was good. Dolph said what we thought was goodbye, gave a wave, and clambered back into the truck and pulled the cord below the rear view mirror blasting the air horns in an annoyingly long and loud salute to the boys. As he turned the ignition, the Bros tape he had clearly been waiting for an opportunity to play, hoping that the listeners would be impressed, blasted across the rastplatz. 'When will I be famous' alas did not do it for the boys, instead they looked away in disgust. Taff looked at Michael the German and asked, "is he Gay?"

Seconds later we were diving into the cars revving the engine and wheel spinning off into the sunset.

The Consallo's

The Consallo family were having dinner in their breakfast room contemplating the weather, Alana's new horse, the stable hand who has taken a shine to Alana, the price of horse tack these days, why they couldn't buy proper buffalo mozzarella in England and other normal concerns dominated their conversation over food and wine. Mrs Consallo asked her husband how business was as he seemed a bit distant recently.

"Darling you know I don't like you asking about my business, it only upsets you if you think I work too hard," he replied. "How is Alana doing at school by the way?" Quickly changing the subject. He did not want to answer and tell his wife about the polyhalite fields which were causing grief.

The phone rang in the kitchen and Mrs Consallo left the table to answer it,

"Darling it's your solicitor can't remember his name, with some good news he says"

"Hallo "

"Yes Michael, it's me, you must go to my office immediately and sign the contract for the land deal, it's through and has been passed by the people at the top, and it's yours Michael, congratulations, well done!"

A huge sense of relief fell on Mr Consallo followed by a feeling of elation. This was the deal of the century, worth millions just for the planning permission for the houses and the shopping centre, but what about the polyhalite and its implications, what of that indeed. Michael hoped it would not be a problem. He rang the investigations company he used and informed them that no further work was needed as the contract was to be signed.

Michael drove to the solicitors office in the Maserati sports car he saved for weekends and the like, feeling good about himself. He put his right foot down more than usual through the dual carriageway passing every car and giving a quick flash of the lights to let the other cars in his way to pull over, a man on a mission was coming through.

K-Team

"Taff you prick. Will you give the cigarette lighter a rest already! It doesn't work, even the next door neighbours blind daschund knows that. You have been faffing about with that plug for god knows how long with no success."

"Listen boyo, do you want a brew or don't you? It's like this you see, that there cigarette lighter has a twelve volt feed to it and I am trying to obtain the red wire from that feed and botch it onto this travel kettle so we can all have a cup of rose lea is nit."

"Ken there's smoke coming from behind the dashboard for fucks sake Taff you nobber, pull over Michael before we all set on fire"

All three of us in the car looked at Taff with the most disappointed face, a face that said why you could not wait fifteen more minutes till we get to the next rastplatz then we could stretch our pins and chill with a brew, but no! Mr impatient trying to be clever, trying to be an auto electrician amongst other things, a fireman with a wet blanket on an electrical fire derrr Taff.

As we got out, the bonnet burst into flames. The car was on fire with no extinguishers on the side of the busy road, the four of us trying to get the explosives and weapons out of the boot, and looking like a scene from an episode of the three stooges.
 Even with the dramatic Welshman ramping up the stress factor, we did eventually remove all kit and equipment,

including the portable twelve volt electrical travel kettle that was the cause of it all.

The car was now in full flame and had drawn a huge amount of attention from rubber neckers on the autobahn, which in turn slowed down the average speed from one hundred and fifty kilometres an hour to about forty clicks an hour, absolutely fantastic, and to top it all, look who now turned up and pulled in behind us, yes, the polizei who stopped us previously.

"Michael did you call the others to tell them what has happened, or did you leave the comms in the other car when we all swapped cars earlier?"

"I have comms but I am much too embarrassed to call them".

"Guess they are on their own for a while then huh".

"Guess so "

Michael was speaking to the German Polizei for about forty minutes, then the fire brigade told us they had finished their job and the vehicle was safe to move or be recovered by the most expensive recovery company in the whole of west Germany who just happened to reside just around the corner, and would pay the fire brigade kommander a commission for his call. What do you know, here they were with orange hazards flashing, sporting a yellow Day-Glo jacket as before, Dolph (Bros twin look-alike) jumped from his wagon with a cheesy grin the size of a prize gorgonzola,

"Oh Gott, was Haben uns here "

"Michael will you just tell that gay boy bros twin to fuck off with his inane looks and effeminate antics and get that piece of scorched metal out of here, dankeshern, and how are we going to get back on our way".

"Well my Polizei friend here will give us a lift to the next rastplatz. There is a car hire company who will have a car there ready for us; his other colleague has called ahead"

"Top banana, so has he got room for our tackle in his car"

"Tackle was is en das?"

"Equipment guns and the like over yonder that pile of shit there"

"Oh err ya Ich hab forgessen das."   (I forgot about that)

We moved all our kit into the Polizei patrol wagon which fortunately was a large estate vehicle that could carry our kit with Taff squashed in the back underneath the now broken parcel shelf acting small like. Walter the Polizei Man drove us approximately four kilometres to a large rastplatz where true to his word was a car hire representative waiting. The representative was five feet ten give or take and had long hair draped over their shoulders down to the chest area, at this point we could not tell what gender this person was as they were quite far away, however they wore a Blitz car hire uniform identifying them as an employee of a small local car hire company recommended by Walter.

"Guten tag mein Herren, Ich hab ein ganz neues auto fur sie, es ist ein Opel Astra, komme sie mit bitte"

"Michael is he taking the piss, a bloody Astra, what are they 1.2cc seventy horse power heap of shit? How are we going to keep up with the rest of em with that snail!"

"I know not what is taking the piss? Man! We must take this and maybe change again depending on the targets location, remember they are in einen van es ist gut fur yetz".

"Bloody have to be won't it "

The cross gender long haired car hire rep walked us over to a small unit with office attached and there it was a brand new sparkling Opel / Vauxhall Astra not a blemish or dent on it.
He gave us the key and said the central locking doesn't work it never did from the factory and there was a recall on it which hasn't been done yet, also the petrol cap is very tight to undo but not tighten, an apparent design fault. But the tank was Harry Toppers and would get us apparently approximately maybe almost three hundred kilometres, Auf Deutsche!

"Connal, how on earth are you going to get in that back seat there you lanky Irish person?"
"Ah well you see that's a good question deserves a good answer, and the answer is put the back seat down flat, move the front seat forward, and I'll plonk myself horizontal like and get some well-deserved zzzz,s"

"Oh you will, will you, that's what I thought you might do being the kind and considerate person that you are, how about we just throw you on the roof and tie you down with a couple of ratchet straps which we could borrow from your Bros twin friend. You Prick"

The miniscule boot of the Astra was opened and all the kit was once again moved from one place to the other, and because of the importance and delicate nature of some of the articles, the equipment had to be removed and replaced two or three times before the packing was perfectly spaced evenly and correctly in such a way that all of it could fit in.

"Taff I just can't believe you are even thinking of taking that, just bin it."

"You must be joking boyo, don't you want a cup of tea then, I've had this travel kettle for about seven years I have, haven't I, it just wants a slight repair to the wiring at the end of the plug there don't you know, come in handy this will, I'll squash it in somewhere, don't you worry".

I looked up into the sky for help and Connal shook his head from side to side whilst looking down at the floor in disgust, Michael the German was desperately looking and hoping that there was no cigarette lighter in the car!

Connal ended up in the front seat driving along with co-pilot Taff to advise, assist and help keep the Irish man awake, not entirely sure if Taff was capable of that task, exciting conversation was not his forte, however he was an absolute whiz at directions and other important useful knowledge.

We had passed signs for Düsseldorf and Duisburg and now were seeing signs for Antwerp and Eindhoven, had no sign of the other car and were waiting for Michael to regain radio contact with the others. All that was to be seen was a busy road with fast cars constantly flashing their lights in our rear view mirror to get out of the way as they wanted to pass. We were travelling at one hundred and ten kilometres an hour, which I am told was fast for one of these pieces of shit, that didn't even have air conditioning or central locking .

Michael had his earphones on this time hoping to catch a response from the other car, but nothing, as yet we were travelling down the Autobahn not knowing where we were going.

"Michael, have you heard from Captain Black recently "?

"Sheisse, halten die klapper mench, Ich kan nicht horren"

I guess Michael was saying be quiet, must have heard something or someone mumbling summat. There were moments of silence as we all knew or thought that Michael was in the middle of something.

"Sheisse, ok Connal please you must continue towards Antwerp, Ghent then Calais, the target car is approximately one hundred clicks away, so how you say put a monkey on it"

"You mean put a Crocodile on it, Michael, make it snappy"!

"Yah naturlich, "Crocodile auch (as well)"

"Captain Black has just said that we are to follow them onto the ferry if they get on it but by no means let them notice us."

"Excellent we shall get drunk again have some pizzas and chill methinks"

"I think I might just buy a paper and read all about it"

"Read all about what Taff"?

"Whatever is happening out there, haven't seen any news or owt recently, bin busy haven't I, so I have. I miss not knowing what is going on in the world, I always used to go down the library and read a meteorology book then a few papers in the foyer and then talk very quietly to the young girl behind the counter about her maths homework, I know her Mum you see, on the account of us living next door to each other a few years previous don't you know."

"Bloody hell Taff I don't know how you coped , the winter nights must have just flown by,   all the excitement, makes me wonder why you joined up in the first place, not sure if I would want to leave all those heart pumping activities behind."

There was an uncanny moment of silence and then;

"You taking the piss Boyo"

"Have you fixed that travel kettle yet or what I'm gagging here"?

"No"

"Michael this heap of shit car feels like it's on its arse, and Connal, will it not go any faster, one hundred and ten clicks an hour will take us about three weeks to get there, and the less time I have to sit next to this Welshman the better."

"By the way Michael, how upset will the Captain be about the Audi being barbequed"?

"You will be able to ask himself in maybe a half hour , see that helicopter up there, he is in that, and will meet us at the next convenient place"

Michael quickly pointed in the direction of the cars glass sunroof to a black blob that resembled a Huey flying above us at perhaps two thousand feet. The slightly frosted and tinted glass roof distorted the figure of the aircraft, so an attempt to clamber over Taff to look at the object in the sky ended up in a miniature street brawl in the back seat of the Astra. The seats being as small as they were, did not cope with the abstract body movements of us both attempting to escape each other's play punches. Taff's elbow accidentally rocketed through the back quarter light window, turning the heads of both the driver and the front passenger in disbelief and shock.

"Taff you Menk, how many cars are you going to fuck up? That's two in the space of one hour, are you deliberately trying to sabotage the operation or what? You Prick, why were you pratting about like a seven year old anyway"?

I was in bits trying to restrain myself from splitting my sides, whilst offering Taff a blanket to put around his neck to keep warm. I waited with bated breath and anticipation for the Welshman's explanation of the events which led to the shattering of the re-enforced glass panel fitted in-between the rear post and the door.

"Well it was like this you see, Wheeltrim here decided;

Connal interrupted the flow of words with an abrupt statement,

"Taff shut the fuck up, I'm bored already".

Each one of us reminded Taff how cold it was on average every two point four minutes, not that we wanted him to feel guilty at all but he is a clumsy oaf, all be it a very intelligent one.
The four speed gearbox of the Opel started to whine with the amount of work it was put under, it was clearly underpowered for the job.

Michael told us that he had made contact with the other car and they were now about forty clicks away and had the target van in sight. A sign for Calais appeared on the side of the road that had what looked like dog chew marks on each corner and the figures were shaded and slightly vandalised, a vision of a past war perhaps. The road surface deteriorated rapidly as we continued on our way to the ferry port, pot holes and badly maintained line markings absorbed the light drizzle that had been falling for the last hour. Cars ahead of us bumped up and down on the uneven surface, a journey I would consider not taking again in the back seat of a small family shopper.

Taff now had four blankets wrapped around his neck in an unsuccessful attempt at closing the gap where the glass was and forming a makeshift thermal pillow so at least he could get some shut eye whilst he was annoying everybody with his presence. My head was placed in an awkward uncomfortable position so as to get the required sore neck syndrome but out of the draught.

"Connal is that temperature gauge supposed to be that high in the red?"

"Only twenty five clicks to go fella, it will have to do"

Michael explained that we were to meet a logistics Sergeant from GSG9 at Calais who has arranged with the customs people to allow us to take our gear on board and over the channel, and we were to leave the hire car with him to deal with and return to the company.

We arrived; the car had actually made it! Michael was ruffling about in the boot of the very tired Opel, after several minutes of rummaging about he withdrew a wad of money from a satchel and passed it on to the logistics man, who was heavy set in his own clothes or he let his garments dangle off his shape in such a casual fashion that his appearance was that of an elephant.

"Watcha Mate, how are you crackin on? "

The Australian accent just did not suit this man. He looked like a Viking disguised as a seventies rock star, including the pirate beard with huge sideburns the size of a three piece settee. The John Lennon sunglasses sat on his nose adding to the oddity of his appearance, and the stance of the man consisted of one leg half cocked, whilst supporting the other against the Land Rover Discovery car he was in. The Land Rover was equally as odd. All the rear seats had been removed so he could sleep in the back at a moment's notice or quickly snap up a bivvi corned dog stew, when the stomach required it. He looked the sort of character who would revel in the torture of sleeping with a pussers issue one hundred and seventy percent wool knitted G10 blanket, which in any normal persons opinion should have been outed in the first world war, as they did nothing but make you itch for seventeen weeks and enforce a terrible eczema type rash that had to be covered in talc at every convenient opportunity.

"What in the Roo's ear have ya done to that car window cobber?"

The question was followed with Tommy gun laugh that resembled a continual bad note played from an out of tune trombone.
Michael tried to explain to the Sergeant about the window, Michael had met this man before but neglected to tell us of his strange looks and mannerisms, people needed some sort of preparation to know how to listen to him and look at him without bursting into laughter.

About thirty minutes later we arrived at the ferry port and were quickly led onto a makeshift boarding plank leading to the staff entrance of the ferry, the tradesman entrance so to speak.

All our kit was carefully and correctly packed into five bergens, all explosives were inside the rucksacks and anything too long to fit in were completely covered in Hessian then coated with at least three extra-large black bin liners, tied around tight with olive drab pussers bungees, made to look like nondescript items or at least nothing like an assault rifle or shotgun.

The image of us walking the plank with these huge rucksacks on our backs was that of five humpbacked sasquatches returning from a hunt back to their cave . With bows and arrows slung around there backs, and the spoils slapped on their shoulders and left to dangle and make shape of a small walking tree, the equipment made us look three times as big as we were.

The corridor was fairly thin and we had to walk sideways in some areas so as not to catch any wall hung pictures or posters, light units, dildo rails and the like.   A walk through the galley proved awkward but was the only way through to our accommodation.

We had three cabins booked for six of us, presuming the Captain or Major might join us, well maybe.   Taff pushed the door open and there was Jock sat down on a bed, cup of tea in hand reading a free glossy with some element of non-gossip text in it.

"Where've ya been, ya bunch a wee poofs? I've been sat here playing travel chess on me jacksy and reading this pile of Shite glossy bog paper"

Taff rubbed his cold sore neck, the rest of us looked at him in disgust and despair, heads shaking, unable to drum up the energy to explain in such a fashion that would not be totally embarrassing for the Welshman.

"Jock as much as we would all like to tell you why we are late,   we all think that you should make us a brew and then direct us to the nearest scran platz, because we are all hank Marvin"

Michael the German quickly brought his hands together with a slight clap and rubbed them in delight and satisfaction with what he saw, a freshly made teapot with tea cosy in place.

The van containing the Russians was still in the queue to drive onto the ferry, awaiting the loading of a several Eddie Stobart heavy goods vehicles and their support vans, a convoy in total of eight vans and trucks delayed the loading process only ten minutes, which wasn't too bad considering the size of them. Then a few caravans followed and other large units.

Major Forrester had been invited by the Captain of the Ferry to have free running of the ship. Using his diplomatic status to full extent, the Major placed himself in the Conning tower, glass of best brandy in one hand and binoculars in the other, watching the Russians from a corner of the tower behind a tinted rounded glass observation area. He watched and followed their van onto the ramp until they disappeared underneath. A sip of the drink to celebrate a satisfying no contact exercise that was of course not yet over, and neither Captain Black nor himself yet knew of the destruction of the Audi. Although Michael had left a wad of hush money with the blonde haired blue eyed bros twin look alike recovery chap, and the same was left with the mutating logistics Sergeant to give to the hire company towards damage done to said Opel, an explanation was still due.

"Jock, not only was that the best brew you have ever made, I'm pretty dam sure it's the only one you have made this month, now where's the scran at?"

"Ah you know we are restricted to the ships staff eating area don't you!"

"Whatever, hurry up man, what happened to your co driver anyway?"

"Oh him, he said he had the shits so I left him at the port to take the Audi back at his leisure, sod him lets go eat"

Michael the German ensured both cabins were locked tight with all equipment secure, except for the slush money bum bag, containing Francs, Marks, Pounds shilling and assorted shrapnel for the on-board amusements no doubt, in total approximately fifteen thousand pounds worth of dosh wrapped around his twenty eight inch waist in a belted bag.

We made our way through the corridors following the delicious smell, taking care not to get lost and end up with all of the tourists and Russian's. We did not want to get noticed at this point as it would matter a lot later.

There was plenty of choice at the food counter, it was a sort of self-service affair plenty of fish and fish dishes, not many red meat choices just steak Canadians and sausages, chips and frozen peas.

"What you having Taff? "

"That looks like sea bass there is'nit, think I'll be having the sausages or maybe the tuna steak with new potatoes, in fact what about that there schnitzel with cheesy pancakes err!"

"So you having everything then "

The boys and me left Taff the talking to himself still deciding , still chunnering , still nodding his head in approval of the layout of scran in front of him.
Michael was finishing his food when the walkie talkie type phone thingy bleeped and was answered fairly quickly. Michael informed us we had to meet the Major in the cabins for a brief, was this the time to break the news on the Audi or not? Let's see what mood he was in first.

The Major sat us down in the small cabin and explained that according to the intelligence people the Russians were planning something big in Yorkshire, and our reccy mission had changed. New part one orders were in place, a shoot to kill order on suspicious activity or mischievous behaviour or words to that effect. Live ammo issued and restrain by any means necessary, no duff manoeuvres as from now. Firearms to be carried, but concealed at all times. The Major continued with his spiel for another twenty minutes and finished the brief with a reference to his favourite old school TV police programme as Phil Esterhouse would say.

"Hey, let's be careful out there".

"Err Major Forrester, the err Audi was it insured "?

"What do you mean, Taff: Was "?

"Well, is then, was, is, is it covered for accidents and the like? "

"Do you mean is it covered for something like fire damage Taff?"

"Yes Major, that sort of thing"

"Already sorted Taff, gone to the local scrap yard to be squashed, don't worry about it but it has cost you a round of pizza's when we get on shore. You Prick! "

"Ok, thanks err Major slight problem with that we haven't been paid yet, do we get paid?"

"Ok men listen in, if you all give me your bank account numbers and sort code's, I will arrange for ten thousand pounds credited to each of your accounts, that needs to last you three months.
We are self-funding, which means we get to keep any spoils from our successes.   Any blackmail money or material commodities also come our way, cars etc, there will be bonuses, is that clear, yes thought so"

The Major didn't give us chance to query that and walked off in a rush back to the conning tower.

"Did yah hear that boys, ten fucking grand each! Ken it's more geld than I've earned in the last twelve years, see that, ten fucking thousand macedonites"

"Jock don't forget the bonuses will you"

Jock was still looking up to the sky area for guidance, he came from a low income family and to even think of ten thousand pounds was unthinkable, never mind the bonuses.

"Michael just as a matter of interest what sort of bonuses might we expect to get?"

"Well Wheels, it's like this, there are sometimes items like stereo's or TV's, or even cars that we seize as part of the criminal activity income, or even houses, but you won't get a house. They generally get rented out to pay for expenses and stuff, but I have received several bits of plunder worth about twenty thousand, that's in a year, plus my ten thousand every three months, and I get spending money which is what's in my bottom bag here, this is for you lot also"

"Bum bag Michael, nicht bottom bag!"

"Ya naturlich, mein freund, Arschloch!"

"Errr Michael what does that mean, Arschloch?"

"Es macht nicht, German rhyming slang"   (It matters not)

Jock and Connal were now in deep rapid eye movement power nap mode, size nine and twelve boots both upturned on each of their beds, Connals head slightly tilted to one side facing south south east, but still snoring. Jocks pillow was half under his head and the other half folded over his now long hair and slightly covering his eyes. Big nose and beard left showing.

Taff was quietly talking to himself hand slightly raised over his knee in a lazy can't be arsed fashion, pointing to the empty wardrobe in the room, still about the food I'm sure, or other impressive memories in his cerebral cortex. Michael and I continued to talk about the bonuses and benefits of working in SOK7, the weather, the price of fresh fish and Maggie Thatcher, of all people that woman comes up in a man talk with a German; doh !! Eventually we both fell asleep on our individual copy chesterfields, or more likely Ikeas best methinks.

I woke up with a twinge from the back of my neck, a possible late reaction to the nettle sting I incurred whilst battling with that Russki. I could feel a few lumps but no hard surface spots, should be ok.

"Put the kettle on ya wee poof"

"Jock I thought you were in the land of nod?"

"Well ya thought wrong didn't ya, laddie, mine is a coffee, white one sugar thanks pal"

"You just lie there and chill and don't forget to put both arms behind your head in full relax position will you"

"Oh Yeah I meant to put them there before I said I wanted a brew, thanks for pointing that out you prick"

"Well I can see land out that there round window thingy, I reckon those white cliffs are where we want to be "

"Are you making a brew are you wheels"?

"Yes I'm making a brew, be sure to let the whole corridor know that I am doing that just in case anyone else wants one won't you "

"So five brews then, is it, "?

"Er no seven brews Wheeltrim, looka"

Michael the German spotted Captain Black and Major Forrester walking through the door. Briefcase in one hand and executive packet of More cigarettes in the other. The Major entered the den of iniquity, the room of cool, and the team of highly trained anti kidnap specialists, who by now were chilling out having a brew.

"Ah good morning to you all we arrived just in time then, kettle on the boil is it Wheels?"

"Yes Sir, right away Sir

"Right let's get to it, find me a table to which I can place my dossiers, and my cup of tea, Wheeltrim, prey where it is?"

The Officers continued with the brief which contained pictures of targets, locations of storage holding facilities, properties with map grid reference figures, orders, current position of hideouts and a few letters from family and loved ones for us.

"Taff that envelope you have, give it here a min, "

"But there's nothing in it boyo, it's empty"

"I know that you faggot, just pass it over"

"It stinks, of perfume, who the hell has sent you that, your boyfriend?"

The aromatic envelope was passed around the room; even the Captain and Major had a sniff, everyone exhuming a sigh of elation and delight at the smell of a woman's perfume. All wondering when it was that we had last tasted the aura of being near a girl.

Taff had not yet finished reading the letter, so Jock stood behind him in an attempt to read who the name was at the bottom of the paper.

"Taff you wee Poof, that letters from your Mam, Ken there's more smelly on that bit of paper than in a whore's handbag ya Jessy!"

Captain Black reached to grab the envelope off Taff and in-between restraining to laugh and calm down the boys, he reads the three letters at the bottom of the letter, Mum!

"Taff is this really from your Mum; I'm having serious doubts in your capability as a mature soldier and diplomat in a specialist unit such as this, if you receive scented letters from your Mother"! A hint of tongue in cheek sarcasm was noted in the Captains tone, a moment of humour from the man with the plan, the man who regularly has conversations with the home secretary and other such big wigs. A man of importance to the human race; apparently has a sense of humour!

"Do you actually have an explanation for this Taff "

"Well yes you see it's like this, that name on the bottom of the page, although it reads Mum, it is actually short for another name, the name of a very good friend of mine who I have known for approximately twenty years, from when she moved to Wales from India, she is half Indian and half Norwegian and she is called Mumarina, hence the abbreviation Mum! You see her job of late has been in the perfume sales department at Marks and Spencers, so she feels it necessary to give me samples of what she sells in the form of scented envelopes.

"Oh I see Taff, then why in the second sentence of the letter does it say your Dad isn't feeling so well"?

The Captain had very quickly thought of that question in a deliberate attempt to further wind the Welshman up, the jester he was.
There was no such sentence in the letter, Taff new it and everybody else suspected it, but can Taff pull himself out of this one as equally successful as the previous time, I think not.

"Well Sir, it's like this you see isn't it, my Mother can't get to the opticians in town as regular as she would like, to get new glasses, so that makes it difficult for her to write, so as Mumarina lives four doors away from my family, she pops round every so often just to see how they are and volunteers to write and tell me stuff don't you know."

The Captain looked at the Major and then directed his looks of disbelief around the room shook his head and then realised that he was on a losing battle with Taff the Welshman, so threw the smelly letter at Taff and walked out with the Major in utter boredom.

"See you later lads"

We had to wait until every car had left the ferry and most of the foot passengers had walked off, until we could pack our stuff on our backs and walk the plank onto the platform of the staff exit and off the ferry, at which point we would locate a contact with a mini bus and an AA map of Great Britain, only it wasn't so Great anymore, still raining same as when we left months ago.

We approached a smartly dressed middle aged man who appeared to be unnaturally normal. "Right chaps you have to get yourselves to that address in the folder, it's in Norfolk" A sort of salesman type attire was donned by the man, tie had been recently slackened from around his neck, the black umbrella above his head had seen better days and had at least three perforations across the radius of the material allowing drips of rain to fall on the shoulder of his jacket he had purchased for a previous special event.

"My contact said you had a thousand pounds for me."

Michael reached for the dosh in his bum bag and quickly counted out a bag of sand to hand over. This was for the supply of the mini bus for a month if we needed it for that long. Looking at it I wasn't sure it was worth anywhere near that amount. Each wheel arch of the red ex post office Leyland Daf was excessively corroded, along with the steel wheels that housed almost illegal tyres.

Connal opened the rear door of the van in a gesture of hope to put all the kit inside but, after several attempts and three sentences of foul language later, he ended up throwing his Bergen over the gap where the passenger seat should have been but was not, and clambered over to find a space for himself. Jock and the rest followed, save for Michael who unintentionally volunteered to drive, with Taff in close support as chief co-pilot come navigation specialist.

The key turned followed by a deafening metallic screech that sounded terrible, the engine surprisingly started and sounded healthy enough, there was however an acute odour of duckhams finest from the tailpipe indicating a possible engine fault relating to the piston rings, a common occurrence with this Horse Shit petrol engine.

"Well you have gotta go that way by the post office there on the left boyo isnit,"

"Ok Taff if sure you are"

"Yes that's right left you are"

"Is that left or right then?"

"Left, left isnit, right you are that's it. Carry on down here for about two miles and then we should hit the motorway on the left; right. Shall I get my travel kettle out boys?"

"Hey Michael, are we to follow them Ruskis all the way up to the Hebrides or what?"
Nein, we go to hotel und Essen haben "

"Ok I hope they have a decent shower there, I'm stinkin, need a shave an' all"

"You must not have shave, you must blend in with the locals wear what they wear, do what they do, you are under cover, "

"Yeah no problem but do we have to look like Grizzly Adams all the soddin time!"

"Who is Grizzly Adams, was ist en das?"   (What is that?)

"How do we know where the Ruski's are going then, they could be going to Devon for all we know?"

"The Major has placed a gps tracker on their van while we were asleep on the ferry es ist kein problem"   (no problem)

"Ok let's hit the hotel then,   how much dosh have you got Michael?
"Enough for whatever you want I'm sure"

CONSALLO HOUSEHOLD…..

Michael Consallo began to pull items of clothing from his clothes rail in the walk in wardrobe, a twenty foot by ten foot palace to store garments, shoes, bags and accessories.   Six full length, gold rimmed and framed

[195]

mirrors stood against the wall, they were individual mirrors next to each other but joined in such a way that they appeared seamless, faultless workmanship with which not many can afford. Two Italian leather armchairs were situated in one corner with a small cocktail table separating them, for champagne and the like. This room could be somewhere a bride could get ready for their big day with drunken friends helping, giggling about the Groom and his Brothers bald head. Multiple shoe shelves dominated a door covered area, with a space above for hats and scarves. A secret felt lined drawer was hidden behind a dummy drawer and contained a selection of watches, one for every day of the week twice over. At least four dress watches, silver and diamond shone against the purple smooth material, two divers watches and a pilots watch with rubber straps dominated the space with their size and arrogance.

Michael reached for the jewel encrusted Rolex Oyster Perpetual day date timepiece, a trusted accessory to the two tone wool jacket worn for this day. A day that Michael would travel back to Italy, to his village near Naples, and contact his extended family and request a sit down with the heads of the Family along with a request for additional funds to commence building works on the Lincolnshire project.

Funds had already passed through the solicitor's hands and on to the seller of the land, however millions were still needed, not just the building but the planning and logistics of the project, contractors and sub-contractors and Naples was the place to get it. Money that had come from all directions, illegitimate means or otherwise, it was there and had been for years, in fact since nineteen thirty when the money started to come in from New York, and continued to come in for a long time. The family were always looking for big projects to clean the dirty cash they had stashed in the graveyard behind the house in fake graves.

Michael slipped some casual leather uppers on his feet and walked down the twelve foot wide staircase carrying his small suitcase in one hand and his jacket in the other.

"Alana dear, have you seen your Mum?"

"Yes Papa, she is in the kitchen making some bruschetta for you I think. Can I come with you to Italy next time please Papa"?

"Yes of course. Are you not seeing your friend today, the one with the father in the Army?"

"No, not today"

Michael had said "Of course" as an answer to that question as he had at least seventeen times in the last six months; he knew he would have to take her sometime soon. Michael said his goodbyes to all and walked outside to his chauffeur and limousine in waiting.

"Morning Giles, the car looks nice and clean as always, to the Airport please".

"Off to Naples again Sir"?

"Yes more business to see to".

Giles was a trusted driver who in his past career had driven very high ranking officials, Royalty, members of parliament and other very important people. He had been an instructor of vehicle escape and evasion techniques with the secret service, an expert in his field; he was well paid for his special services.

The first class flight to Naples was a pleasant journey with hardly any turbulence, thus allowing Michael to relax and enjoy a glass of Amarone and flirt with the air hostess called Constance whom he knew from his many trips on this flight. Michael would tease her continually with promises of taking her on a yacht to the sunset over Montego Bay or anywhere in the Bahamas and live the life of luxury. Just the two of them, talking sweet nothings in each other's ear.

The landing at Naples had an air of nobility about it; even the touchdown on the tarmac with the miniscule wheel skid screech sang a song with an operatic Dolby tone. Even with the air conditioning at full throttle, the hot Italian air still managed to find its way into the aircraft and fill the atmosphere with warmth, prompting the passengers to remove non revealing garments so as not to perspire in the heat. The cabin crew were all now at the doors waiting for the portable remote control tunnel to be driven and parked outside the door with seal flaps pressed against the fuselage of the plane, a must before the door could be opened. A steward walked along the tunnel and ensured all safety clips and measures were applied and enforced, he then signalled to Wendy the senior hostess the thumbs up all are in order sign, and the doors opened.

Michael stepped through the tunnel and followed the other passengers towards customs and luggage pick up. It was fast and efficient for a change, and within minutes Michael was in reach of the large glass exit doors where he could look for his ride to the Avellino Province. His luggage would be picked up by an employee of the family who would bring it to him at the farm estate.

It was Antonio Furillo waiting for him by the open car door, Michael's father's personal driver. Michael gave a little wave and approached the car and shook his hand in appreciation for being here on time. After saying a few polite words about the weather Michael looked around and out of the car window towards Mt Vesuvius, and imagined he was there and overlooking the marvellous bay of Naples. The whole landscape emitted a reminiscent allure, and made Michael realise what he was missing. His eyes followed the landscape across the rolling hills and down towards the Mediterranean Sea, another dream of walking ankle deep in the crystal blue sea , eyes peeled for the next front page " It" girl to appear in Hello magazine. Several local girls had been spotted here in the surrounding different villages such as San Vitaliano, Marigliano and Saviano. Apparently Michael had been told that the population of the Avellino province contained ten thousand more females than males, a fact useful when looking for a potential "second wife" if one was needed.

Approximately forty five minutes had passed when the slight inclination of the long one kilometre drive of the family farmhouse was visible, lined with trees on either side that overhung in the middle forming a green tunnel, and five foot sunflowers growing in between the tree trunks made the driveway appear slightly kaleidoscopic with a quick unconcentrated squint from an unfamiliar eye. The guarded electric gate closed behind the limousine whilst the tyres on the heavily varnished stone flags clicked on each revolution, increasing the speed of the car reduced the time lapse of the clicking and eventually became unnoticeable.

Armed guards became visible nearer to the house. They surrounded the beautiful three hundred year old farmhouse with a curtain of security, protecting the family members from attempted assassinations and burglaries. There had been several recent hostile attempts to gain access to the grounds and its habitants.

The car came to a stop. Michael got out and knew that everyone would be round the back sitting at the seventeen foot dining table that overlooked the swimming pool. He could now see smiling faces and men standing up from their seats eager to meet him.

HOTEL.   K-TEAM

"I canni understand why I'm on stag duty, what have I done wrong"?

"Jock you haven't done anything wrong, it's not your fault you were born in Scotland"

"Shut it Weazel ya wee poof, before I remove your larynx and pretend it's a haggis "

"Jock it's only for a few hours, all you have to do is sit by the window, gat in hand and watch for any odd goings on, simples insnit boyo, if you like you can try and fix my portable travel kettle while you have a minute."

"Taff, yer aff yer heid mon if ya think am gan anywhere near that fire hazard piece of shite, it wants wazzin in the bog ya bampot."

"You can think about it, if you like Jock, might keep your brain working for a short while"
"Ken the only thing that is gonna keep my brain working is to not listen to your welsh valley shite Mon"

"I guess I'll have a look myself shall I "

"You shall "

Jock walked off muttering and cursing to himself, disgusted that he had been volunteered for first stag.

He found the corner that contained all the equipment and routed out the best defence weapon he could find which was a Heckler Koch 416 assault rifle with 10 inch close quarter barrel fitted and infra-red target light attached. Looked good, didn't weigh much in comparison to others, and had a fire rate of about eight hundred rounds a minute provided you were able to make like an octopus with the magazine changing.

This rifle being standard issue of the Grenzschustzgruppe (GSG9) a counter terrorism and special operations division of the German police force formed in nineteen seventy three, of which Michael the German had been an operative for some years now, and still had never worn any uniform of any kind except for combat and camouflage wear of black origin, pay was good and got to travel extensively; Happy as Larry.

Jock placed the rifle in his right hand, picked up a cup of coffee in his left and kicked the chesterfield type hotel room chair one hundred and eighty degrees to face out the window and plonked himself in it. The leather chair made a long fart noise under the weight of the man with the grizzly adams beard, prompting a turning of his head towards all of us with one eyebrow lifted in Roger Moore style. Expecting a series of complaints from the boys, he was both relieved and disappointed that we had already adopted schlaf (sleep) mode and were in the never ever land of nod. Moments later Jock was the same.

The morning sky cast a light ray through a gap in the curtain right into Jock's face and eventually annoyed the hell out of him. He opened one eye and gruntled some undercurrent Scottish curs vocabulary, fortunately nobody was yet awake to hear him and ask what language he was talking. Jock lifted one leg up and pointed it towards the curtain, sliding his bottom along the chair but not changing his almost comfortable sleeping position, the leg with pointed foot then attempted to move the curtain to the left in a wild stab at closing the gap to stop the light shining through. The ballerina foot movement failed miserably, undeterred, Jock lifted his leg and tried again. He could not move his posterior any further to get closer to the curtain because that would have moved his stomach which was still supporting the cup of undrunk coffee from last night. The curtain rings began to slip along the rail with the fabric ever so slowly following.

"Jock what are doing?"

Jock was totally unaware that there was anyone up and about never mind right behind him, the slightest noise would make him jump out of his skin.

"Ya fuckin wee Bassa, shite, soddin ell, Ken there's coffee all oer me pants now ya wee poof , I wus tryin to shut the curtain so the light didn't wake you all up; Wheeltrim !"

"Jock I don't know why you didn't use that bed over there it's much more comfortable"

"What"

"We were only kidding when we said you had to stag on you nutter, but it was a good craic listened to you chimf about it"

"You twats, Michael were you in on that, I don't bloody well believe you lot have done that you set of cunts, you had better get the kettle on before I blow ma heed Mon. Wankers!!"

Captain Black walked in the hotel room and of course enquired what all the rumpas and commotion was about, and was informed that Jock went to sleep with a cup of coffee on his lap and spilt it because he fell asleep in that chair for some weird reason.

"What on earth did you fall asleep in the chair for Jock, there is a perfectly serviceable pussers bed there, you nob"

"Well Sir these tosspots told me I had to be on stag on last night and look out the window."

"So you fell asleep while on guard duty Jock did you? Court martial offence that you know, might I suggest that all this will be forgotten after you have made everyone a cup of tea, you prick!"

The Captain had a particular way of making somebody do something without having to give an order and he had a certain flair about his speech when doing so, a certain nobility when he added the word prick onto every statement, a definite trait of university education.

"Ok lads we have a short break of approximately fifteen hours according to our inside man, the Russki's are thirteen miles away in a disused warehouse preparing for something big, not sure what yet but it involves about twenty five people in total and is going to take place somewhere in Yorkshire we think. Get plenty of food, sleep, women whatever you want but make sure you are ready to go from here at zero three hundred hours tomorrow, one of you will need to drive at that time."

RUSSIAN WAREHOUSE

"Boris you have weapons, yes?"
"Yes, but I do not have map to Harrogate, do you have it, and picture of girl?"
"Ya here is picture"

"Nice, how old?"

"I do not know, does it matter?"

"Niet"

"Ok, you and the other two must meet the other five at this address, we have people watching the farmhouse at the moment, and the father has gone somewhere on a plane so that is better, we must do this as soon as he gets back so we must be prepared and ready, with all escape plans in place. There is also a form to pick up from that house when you meet the others, it is a land rights register form, just get it signed by the man, the Father, when you have the girl you know what to do".

The Russians had been planning this mission for a long time; this included the technical sample scientists who took samples in the fields in Lincolnshire, the game of golf with Michael Consallo, the movement to England of individuals taking part. All set up for this, the possession of a very important plot of land worth millions to the right people. The mineral polyhylate would get shipped back to Russia and used to form part of massive money making conglomerate of the "Solntsevskaya Bratva" the brotherhood of organised crime in Moscow. Approximately seventy soldiers were involved in this mission, not a scratch on the membership of nine thousand. Very organised, very efficient, very powerful and very dangerous, how could a team of about six handpicked Special Forces trainees and their assistants prevent these men and women from achieving their goal. Minor miracle perhaps or maybe just good old true British bulldog grit!

"Boris, go organise some pizzas or chips or some other shit English food we are all hunger here "
"Ok, I go to the chip shop it is gut there, da ist a blonde woman who works there, she likes me, gave me free sausage last time Ya"

"Boris here is keys for BMV, the blue one"

"They are all blue"

"Boris you fucking asshole, go get food, knobhead dickface, use the car that the key fits idiot kurwa". (Bitch)(Polish)
"I have fucking clowns for soldiers, can't even see what colour cars are, and I have to eat fucking shit English pommes frits, let's get this job done and finish, go home ".

Boris came back with a huge bag of cold chips and fish which were two portions short and no diggers or tomato ketchup, and so gained the proud accolade of nob of the day.

Food was distributed unevenly and untidily and rotational shifts were placed in front of the microwave, as one man could not multi-function enough to cope with warming seventeen newspaper wrapped portions of chips; A woman however may have managed slightly better but would have moaned for the rest of the week about the smell of fat under her nails, or the black and white newspaper print transferring on to her skin, so this job almost definitely was best left to the men to struggle and complete alone.

After the feast there was a gathering of equipment and people to get ready for the trip to Harrogate, then a meeting at the round table which had appeared out of nowhere, orders were given, escape and evasion techniques to be used as taught at the training headquarters of Solntsevskaya bratva Participation of Extortion, Counter Terrorism, Revenge and Extremism (SPECTRE).

The majority of the equipment necessary for the task in hand was contained in the lead van as the convoy set off from the warehouse and was the one that had a homing device planted on it at a service station in Germany by none other than Major Forrester. This was closely monitored by our surveillance team who followed them at a range of thirty miles, who in turn conveyed the location to Michael the German, who in turn, as and when he thought was necessary, informed us, hoping we would act on our initiative and carry out standard ordinary practice required.

Two other fast cars followed the van out onto the main road at an approximate speed of fifty five miles per hour, not quite the maximum speed limit, but just enough not to arouse the suspicion of the local traffic patrol.

Michael the German thrashed out a verbal command instructing us to get our shit together quick style (Schnell machen) as he had word of the Russians movements, the hotel, the night out, the pizza, the beers and the potential woman hunt had to go on the back burner, we were out of here and off up the road, northbound Yorkshire way, now! The first thing I thought of when Yorkshire was mentioned, was calling in at the Skipton pork pie shop, best pork pies on the planet! Alas time would not be on our side, a note of urgency was the mojo of the day and emitted an air of excitement about the atmosphere, action, adrenaline, danger and most of all a chance of revenge on the Russian rugby tackle Sasquatch who felled me in a bunch of good old Urtica Dioica and gave me an itchy neck for about a week.

A speed of ninety miles an hour was quickly reached in the horse shit van supplied by the suit and boot, it rattled and hummed as though the engine was about to fall out or the suspension was about to come off but oddly enough we thought it was sure to get us there inconspicuously as required. All our voices had to be raised due to the noise of the donkey under the bonnet and the smell of burning oil crept into the cabin forcing us to block our noses. At this speed, that noise and the horrific odour we were sure to be travel sick within fifteen minutes.

"Here Taff pass me that first aid kit will ya man"
"What's wrong with you boyo"

"I need to see if there is any Brufen in the pack, I feel sick or anything to get rid of this headache"

"Eye, Ken hurry up Taff you prick I have a fod eache too Mon"

Taff rummaged around digging deep into the green kit bag and felt a round cylindrical shaped object thought to be the container housing the pills, plasters and such like, it was tight in the kit bag, stuck on something. Taff tried to move the jarred items from inside the bag and separate the kit from its surrounding friends.

A tight grip and a sharp tug and then a warp speed arm movement finally freed the item. So much speed in the limb movement that Taff's arm thrust itself into the roof of the van and the canister ejected itself from his hand and flew into the frame of the window, then ricochet towards the van floor. The canister landed rather abruptly and began rotating rapidly like a mutant spinning jenny, our ears could hear a hissing noise, a release of pressure from somewhere perhaps, yes it was coming from the canister, it was not the first aid kit after all it was a more sinister item of importance.

"Taff now what the fuck have you done ya dozy welsh twat!"

We all looked at each other in complete amazement, a moment of silence ensued and then Connal started inadvertently laughing at nothing other than the fact that not only had the canister stopped spinning but had started to move slowly in a backwards motion with the force of the escaping gas. One after the other we all started laughing and pointing at each other, not able to explain why we were all in stiches over a can on the floor that had a mind of its own. All of a sudden all of our voices changed tone to a high pitched pig oink squeal which forced out more childish giggles and abstract limb movements. Arms rose abstractly dangling in mid-air looking for the strings, like a scene taken from an episode of thunderbirds perhaps or maybe a squad of special government agents in a van sniffing nitrous oxide.

Jock picked up the can and tried to read off the side of it, N20 do not puncture or store in a hot or warm place.

"Taff you clown I can't stop laughing, my headache has gone, did I even have one, what is the weather doing is it snowing, I can see white things, I don't remember if I cried when if watched ET "

Fifteen minutes of inane delirious verbal comments and drunken like body movements .made us come to the conclusion that the canister on the floor of the van was not the first aid kit but was in fact a canister of Laughing gas.

"Are we there yet?"

"Are we there yet?"

"Here Taff, how come somebody with so much brains and knowledge like your good self can be so ridiculously shite in a car, for example every car I have been in with you has been either trashed beyond recognition, burnt, smashed, damaged in some way or from just by the plain and simple fact that you are in it, being you? You can't even make a brew safely, you could have brought a flask like everybody else, but no, how long have you had that relic of a travel kettle with the now modified crocodile clip connectors soldered on with a Brule torch you found in the safe house. The first thing I am going to do when we get to the next service station is buy you a new one so you can bin that piece of scrap, it's the main instigating problem with you and any car you decide to travel in it is a jinx man!. Are you this much bad luck back in the valleys"?

"I want to keep my crocodile clips Weazel, I'll put them back in my Welsh survival kit which I have had for about fifteen years, which was given to me by my Grandad, who obtained it during the war"

"Whatever, Michael can I have some dosh at the next services please?"

"Ya aber Sie haben es yetz, so Ich nicht forgessen "(have it now so I don't forget)

"Bloody 'ell, one hundred quid! That will do cheers r kid"

"Ya das ist for essen auch " (that is for food as well)

So McDonalds for all of us that will be about forty five sov's, then a paper, a few stickys (sweets) for the journey, two bottles of pop and water, then off to the gadget shop for a travel kettle for my mate Taff.

"Connal, are we there yet, the services I mean, how far?

THE RUSSIANS.

The Kolorov brothers were talking together with two other of the kidnap team, discussing how they would obtain the daughter of this millionaire then take her to a place nearby while they forced the Father to sign the rights of the southern half of the land, the agricultural aspect of it, to the Russian Company named "Moshkovich Minerals", which was a shell company indirectly owned by SPECTRE. This company had the facilities to contract out the necessary workforce to ship out, and manufacture the mineral polyhalite into Russia in the form of inorganic fertiliser, which had a massive revenue potential across the country.

The Russians were experts at spotting potential illegal forms of obtaining other people's fortunes. Even though this would not affect the building of houses on the plot, it would be more rewarding, and could be delivered across several parts of Russia filling the pockets of many of the distributors and most of all, the money vaults of the Solntsevskaya Bratva.

"So you are confident you can get girl, take her to this house here, then ring me when you have the father in custody, ya?"

"Ya no problem all is good, Boris has organised transport and Dorsky and Karl are with me in the land Cruiser with tools. But I have to give the boys a little cash money to keep them going as there is none till we have finished the job."

"Ya here have this wad! I think there is five thousand there, divide it equally between them and tell them to stop being such women".

"All is good"

"Ok get ready, we move out in thirty minutes".

Ten minutes had passed, and the Land Cruiser was now at the front of the property on the tarmacked drive with two hired white Transit vans behind neatly parked up ready to go. Each of the team was either in the toilet getting rid of all the vodka from last night or having a last fag and a laugh with each other before the journey to the farmhouse at Harrogate   Dorsky repeatedly walked around each vehicle checking all tyres had enough air in them to not give any trouble, and then he opened the rear doors to the vans and checked all weapons were easily accessible and ammunition nearby, masks, tape, tie wraps and rope at the ready. There was also a supply of chloroform to calm and put to sleep any irate Mum's or other.

A grunted order from Boris made the team enter their vehicles and start the engines, a convoy of kidnappers, a movement of terror, a logistical horror.

THE K-TEAM VAN

"Put your foot down Weazel, you Jessy"

"What is Jessy "? asked an intrigued Michael the German.

"A Jessy is a dork faced, button brained, doughnut called Whealan who thinks driving at thirty miles an hour on the motorway is sufficient to catch the Ruski's, Wheels you dog's breath put a crocodile on it!"

"I'm trying,   this thing is taking three days to get past forty for some reason, and there is a burning rubber smell, or burning something smells."

"Eye and it's coming from the back end man, what 'n'the hoot has gan on"?

"It's brakes isnit boyo, that's what it is, isnit. The brake linings are catching another part of the system thus creating friction and heat and the end result being overheating, smelling brakes and possible restriction of movement of at least one of the wheels at the back, yes that's what it is"

"Taff thanks very much for that expert diagnosis, but perhaps you could enlighten us all on the remedy of the said problem before we catch fire, again."

"Ah well what you have to do is stop the car, remove the wheel where the problem is unstick the sticky thing, er, er, er, oh clean it put it back together and that's what you do isnit. Or you could just stop the car, shove it in reverse and jolt it backwards a few times at a rapid rate of knots that generally does the trick"

I put the car into neutral and pulled over on the hard shoulder of the M1 motorway, the car slowing down fairly quickly on its own with its sticky thing brakes, the van ground to a halt. Reverse gear was selected, clutch released and the van jolted backwards, skidded a few times, then a clunk sounded and hey presto that was that.

"Right get on with it Man, put thee clog down"

The team addressed their weapons and equipment, and made sure all webbing had the relevant magazines in their correct pouches and were ready to sling around shoulders at a seconds notice. Taff picked up this Star Trek looking type of binocular affair, with attachments and dangly bits attached, looked at it turned around a few times, not really knowing which way round it was supposed to be or what bit went where. He scratched his head a few times then attempted to attach it to his belt, in the hope that someone would stop him and tell him what it was and where it went.

"Taff you Clown, what the fuck are you doing to that set of night goggles? They fold up and go in your breast pocket of your smock you prick".

"Yeah I know that don't I, I was just trying something else."

"Oh my God Taff, I thought you knew everything about everything as well, Derrr, did the Library at home not have a book on night vision equipment then"

"Well it did, and I read it but it just kept me in the dark didn't it boyo"

"Yes I can see that, give it here you wazzak, what you do with this is you put that dangly bit on the front of that dark tinted screen, then you put that plug into there, then you wrap that other dangly bit around that Velcro bit there and pull the strap out a bit and place the whole apparatus around your bonce and then turn it on, like so."

"Ken, you fatha a six foot extra-terrestrial wasp with that piece of shite on ya heed ya wee poof". How the feck are ya supposed to feet with that on Mon? "

"Well Jock it's like this, the piece of apparatus is used for night vision, that means it can make you see in the dark , with that in mind the user of the equipment in question is at an extreme advantage him or her being able to see, you see.

Therefore the enemy not being able to see is more vulnerable and might not see you do a sneaky beaky on him and render him into deep schlaf mode, do ya see Jock?"

"Fuck off Weazel ya nob"

"Taff will ya remove that headgear and get busy with that Ganz Neau deluxe ghia model travel kettle that I have just spent Her Majesty's coin on just for so you don't blow any more vehicles up with it"

"I'm just unwrapping it as we speak man, there are instructions here, that's a start, there is the actual kettle itself, but where is the plug? There is no soddin plug on it the wankers, it's missing! Bloody 'ell Weazel trust you to get the one with the missing part, looks like a catalogue return jobbie been thrown in with the unmarked models by mistake, isnit boyo, what a bloody rip off man. I don't believe that someone can pack that together without putting the lead in. Shit, I knew I should have kept my other one, at least it had a lead with it."

"Taff the lead from your kettle killed the car"

"Yeah but, no but Yeah"

The travel kettle was passed around just to make sure the lead wasn't hidden inside or in the top or.

"Taff, pass that box over here a minute "

Taff picked up the box and tossed it towards the inquisitive Michael, and during mid-flight the box revolved and another small box dropped out of it. The two boxes mysteriously landed on each knee of the GSG9 agent, prompting him to discard the one Taff had already looked at. He picked the other one up, turned it upside down and shook it about. A perfectly rounded, moulded kettle base shaped plastic object dropped onto his already left foot.

"Aha, was ist en das mein frieund?" (What is that my friend)

The fallen article was in fact the travel kettle base that formed the cordless description on the front of the box that had been discarded, the base had a lead protruding from the rear lowest point through a groove in the base, there was also a steel bracket sellotaped to the inner part of it, to attach the base to a dashboard or similar, with screws. The lead also had two ends at one end, one was a universal car cigarette lighter plug, and the other had two convenient crocodile clips attached, soldered and screwed. Completely and utterly Taff proof. PERHAPS!

"Taff is that bloody thing plugged in yet ya fanny?"

Taff gently and gingerly like probed the universal plug into the twelve volt socket situated just below the non-operational radio, and the green on light illuminated to the delight of the cabin crew.

Taff how long does it take, is it boiled yet?"

"No but it looks like it is having a good go at being nearly there, find some pussers G10 mugs boyo!"

Two of the team searched the kit bags for the mugs but were disturbed by the back door suddenly opening and flirting itself around its hinges whilst banging itself against the outer rear wing panel of the van.

"Grab a hold of that soddin door man"

Connal and I attempted to secure each other to the van and retrieve the van door; Jock meanwhile had been instructed by Michael the German to find a bungee to use as a door securing device. There was now an elasticated door stay strap at full stretch holding and securing the rear door which ran from the base of the front seat through the centre of the rear seats to the hinge lock on the door, thus creating a perfect twanging weapon on the person opposite's knees.

"Here Taff how far do you think I would have to pull this bungee back to embed it in your welsh kneecaps?"

"About as far as I would throw you out of that back door with the bungee unattached Weazel!"
"Michael that burning oil smell is back, are we there yet?"
The Russians were sat down, smoking, talking, resting on a slightly inclined grassy knoll in a lay by just off the M1 near a cafe discussing the route and the recce before the kidnap, they would spend three hours preparing, planning and double checking each other's jobs and at what time they had to be done. The first one was to call the house and ask for Mr Consallo to make sure he was in, then in turn the men would systematically surround the

house, then one man dressed as a delivery man would knock on the door, force it open and let the others in, secure the house, cut the phone line, grab the daughter, tie up the parents and do one.
Simples!

"Right Boris go gather men, have piss, shit and we go!

K-TEAM VAN;

"Michael, shit it's them, look they're just getting into their vehicles, the Russki's "

"No shit Sherlock, have you only just spotted them, keep focussed don't look at them, you most of all Wealtrim as you have met already with the nettles fight before."

"Ok I will scootch down and hide a while until you park, or do we follow? "

"Nein, we stay until further instructions from Captain Black. We must have all of them together and in a position to which they might be threatening to other people, in other words in a state of arrestable condition, as in with weapons in hand about to commit a crime."

Within seconds of parking in a quiet inconspicuous designated parking position in the lay by, a plain clothes police traffic car pulled up next to us, two doors opened and out got two police men. We could tell they were police by the luminous stripes they wore across their lapels and diagonally across their chests, not exactly noticeable from outside the car but definitely in your face. Look at me I'm a man in charge wearing a ridiculously looking gay outfit with dayglo village people style stripes across my flat chested torso, whilst attempting to give it the macho "I AM " look. Coupled with a moustache that resembled a vision from a random homesteader in 1879 and huge nose to boot, both, er , MEN approached the van.

Connal looked at me, I looked at Jock, Jock looked at Michael and Taff whispered to us all,
"Are these two for real?"

"Evening all"

A high pitched squeaky voice struggled to be emitted past the fur on the policeman's mouth and chin, a slight nervousness prevented the voice from sounding like anything other than a teenagers unbroken speech tone, which was odd because this, er, man appeared to look about thirty plus years old. He had long chimpanzee arms too, outstretching the police issue fleece he wore, now his oppo on the other hand looked almost the part with the same attire but his moustache was a lot neater and more fitting to his huge mouth and didn't cover his nostrils as much.

"We have been following you for approximately three miles and during that time your rear door flung itself open three times, thus creating a danger to yourself and other road users therefore it is my duty as a road traffic police officer to inform you that we intend to arrest you in the name of the law!"

We all looked at each other again and again and used telepathy to ask ourselves, "are they taking the Piss"

"We must first ask you all your names, and what is your business here on this road "

"Have you got any ID pal "

I felt I must ask the question to the policemen, because the appearance of these two was not of anything I had seen before. Jock looked at me and nodded in approval, and telepathically transferred a; "I'll get you a beer later for that one as it deserved such a reward."
"ID"?

"Yes it is a way of proving who you are and what you do, we have ID cards don't we guys, and if you show us yours we will show you ours"

I was not sure if that sounded a bit gay but it seemed to do the trick, out popped two ID cards with the Queens badge on with respective pictures corresponding to each police person, not policeman or policewoman, just police person, as we were not sure which these were.

"Taff have you got your ID card on you Pal?"

"Yeah I reckon so Wheels!"

"Right there we are! Two ID cards for your perusal"

I allowed them to see what was written on the cards and just before their faces dropped I spoke the proverbial sentence,

"We are on important confidential business and must on all accounts be allowed to continue on our way!"

The police persons obviously had never seen these ID cards before with the word Diplomat in capital letters all over them. They looked at each other for a short while and decided it best to pass back the cards and politely asked us to fix the revolving van door at our earliest convenience and be on our way.

A voice projected rearwards from the front passenger seat turning all heads. In a we must listen immediately and act now tone,

"Taff will you sort that bloody door out ya wee poof "!

Jock was getting a bit fed up of listening to the door clatter against the hinge, even though it was bungeed up and sort of secure. It was still squeaking and twinging and making an excruciating, irritating noise against the corroded and discoloured steel hinges and handle mechanism, normally used to close and lock the door.

The journey was just about getting a bit tedious to say the least, however Michael had managed to repair the factory fitted wireless (radio) and successfully located a radio channel that gave half decent reception. The music was terrible and in mono sound but just about muted the noise from the door.

"Any news on the blower from Captain Black by the way"?

"Ya, I have news, hand me the map bitte (please)"

The map was passed over, and a complete look of disgust appeared on Michaels face as he tried to unravel the incorrectly folded map. No longer was it in a perfectly formed concertina fashion, more of a folded in half seven times and then placed in a book to smooth the creases out and then placed at the bottom of the pile order.

"What's up Michael?"

"I cannot read the maps because it has nicht been folded correctly "

Michael continued to shake his head for a further what seemed like ten minutes in dismay and then;

"Captain Black has instructed us to park this van at this address and then how you say er yomp with equipment to this area here and scrim up and observe this house here and wait for further instructions."

We all looked at the equipment that filled the van and then looked at the two bergens (rucksacks) that were now empty from when we were bored and started to check everything, and thought that we will need at least another three bergens to comfortably manage a yomp through unknown terrain, for an unknown period of time.

"Er Michael how the fuck are we supposed to get from said A to said B with all this shit here plus provisions to go? "

"Ahh, we will need a stop first at the next services, I think we meet someone with more bergens and food/drink and shit"

"Well good, cause I need some more socks".

"Connal you need more than a pair of socks pal".

The journey continued for about an hour with all noises good and bad, and Michael pulled over at the parking spot and pointed to the brow to the north.
"Ok, er Connal und Wheels common sie mit" (come with me).

We unattached the bungee cord to allow the exit from the vehicle which forced a final high pitched fingernail on blackboard screech from the door as the full rotation of the rusted aged hinge, causing frictional heat vibrations which made the door just fall off!

"Oh nice one Taff"

"Not my fault is it, poxy bloody heap of shite isnit boyo. I said poxy bloody heap of shite man, I didn't get where I am today by travelling in heaps of Shite all bloody day long"

"And where are you today Taff?"

"I'm here boyo, very annoyed, sat next to an annoying person who is asking particularly annoying questions"

Connal and Jock followed Michael over the brow and into a nearby field. There he was smoking his ceeegar, sat side on, legs propped on the landing skids of the parked Huey helicopter. Captain Black giving it the Jon Wayne again.

"Ahhh there you are men, right got some shit here for you and details as from here on, pay attention this is still a full on mission that's a no-duff operation so got to be on the ball with it, grab these stores and saddle up !"

The Captain slid the two extra bergens from the alloy floor of the Huey and passed them to us, and with an approving "get on with it" nod of the head, twisted his legs into forward motion position and gave the pilot the go-ahead finger semaphore signal. The Huey sparked into life, turbine whistling and rotors turning, that was our bye bye see you later alligator prompt.

The three wise men appeared in sight of the rapidly deteriorating van with an apparent weight on their shoulders. The two bergens the captain had given us were packed to the hilt with shit for the rest of the mission and even Jock looked to be struggling with the weight.

"Piggin ell what on earth is in these bergens, feels like fifty cans of bully beef man, it weighs a soddin ton!"

"Yeah I canni wait ti waz it in the back e that bag a shite van"

"I'm sure it will be most necessary "

Michael had to come out with the end sensible comment being the responsible mature experienced German twat he was. Even though it was annoying it was unfortunately true, the said contents of the rucksack would be most important articles which we needed. We all decided to pile back into the back of the van and get on our way and discover what was inside whilst we were travelling, so the dilapidated door section was whizzed to the side of the road and placed in an unmarked grave with a headstone inscribed, 'Here lies the remains of a pointless piece of metal.'

A few piss stops later Michael read out the next course of instructions as laid out in the document passed on to him by the Captain. It read;

Ditch the van at the lay bay on the road leading of here
Point "A"   Make your way to this eight figure grid reference, dig in at this grid reference,   form a high view reccy point "B" Observe the routine and security at the Consallo Farmhouse point "C" and await further instructions through sat phone.

"Shittin 'ell, does that mean we have to cart this shit how many miles across country Taff?   Sort the best route out for us man, work your oriental skills so we don't have to yomp as far".

You mean orientational skills Wheeltrim"

"Ya Taff that would be ok but we must on all accounts pass through this woodland hut here, there are supplies to pick up and apparently according to this map there is a toilet there with free comfy bum"

"Oh well then that's completely worth yomping about thirty miles over rough terrain carrying seventy kilograms on our backs isnit boyo".

"Taff will you stop being such a Debbie Downer! Have a bit of positiveness about you for a change won't you? Just carry on and think of all those woolly jumpers you can knit at home when we have finished this pullover".

Michael replied, "What is Pullover?"

"Ken, pullover is Wheeltrim givin it large on the Laurel and Hardy lingo, the wee poof, what he means to say is palaver ".

"Ah so, how you say, er Dumbkopf sprechen, thick speak er idiot language, velleicht"   (perhaps/maybe).

"Eye Michael all of the above so it is"

Connal wasn't into saying much but had to have the last word on most occasions.

"Are you sure the Captain said leave this heap of shit here Michael, bloody ell it's in the middle of nowhere, nobody will find it to pick it up, it's nowhere near anything not even any trees or disguise or camo or nothing".

"Exactly!"

We gathered the equipment and split the weight into each other's Bergens sort of evenly. Just Taff that had the extra three boxes of ammo in his, he wouldn't know! We picked up the sheathed gats and shouldered them with the specially newly designed carrying straps.   The new straps were made of such a material that didn't rub into your shoulder and give you neck burn which would rub against your sweaty neck whilst marching to anywhere but where you wanted. All new equipment was on trial to the Marines, other special forces and addons like us also had the opportunity to try out, criticize, and remark on the quality and performance of the said article.

Taff took over the terrain assessment, looked around at a few trees and shrubs as a professor of horticulture would, and as a wild stab in the dark at humour instructed us to dress up camo style with items of local foliage. The Prick!

"Taff ya wee poof man,   wilya fuck off with ya inane suggestions and geet on with the job in hand"

"JOB is a positively disgusting word"
 Connal spoke his one word an hour   allowance in a short second!

"Woahh Connal you have an opinion on the word Job?"

"Aye laddie, it's a terrible one so it is, almost as bad as Meal!! Yak "remind me never to repeat those words again, no, ever again in my whole life for as long as I live"

"Yes I think you have told us once already by the way, here see that,   have a purple heather bush for yur heed mon, match ya straw bonce ya wee poof, now get a move on "

Michael the German was just bewildered at the lingo of us all, not really understanding most of it anyway and throwing the odd polite laugh in here and there, just to let us know he was listening, well of a fashion leastways.

Taff led the way over the hills and far away, ever so confident with his ability to just get there quicker and easier than anyone else, knowing every step would be the right one in the right direction, no map, no compass, just contour appreciation, projective application, "follow me chaps" attitude and a small percentage of luck, and that was that!

"How long Taff"?

"Just over that brow two miles over the other hill and we should see the building where we get a resupply of rations and stuff, there are two buildings apparently, not sure what the other one is yet, one is definitely a farm or farmhouse, the other not sure."
"Ten minutes then".

Michael the German was muttering something in German through the sat phone to someone speaking back in German, (how very odd!), whilst walking at a slower pace than anyone else. Something was brewing we could feel it in our balls, sunshine in our pockets, good soul in our feet, we were raring to go.
Michael finally stopped in his tracks and said nothing, just listened. German speak changed to English receiving and transmitting, we could now understand what was said.
"What's happening Michael me old china"?
"What is happening is that we are to get a move on, things are happening, we have to, how you say, "Put a crocodile under it "ya und we must be sure to stop at the resupply farm on the map".

The weather was a typical autumn evening. Cloud with some sunshine, not too cold and a mild dripping of rain just to make us feel as though we were actually in England not some exotic island in the Bahamas sunning it up with women a plenty, just us waltzing along on the concrete road to nowhere but trouble, it seems!

The two houses came into view. Across two fields and over a small river were situated two separate buildings, one a definite oldy worldly farmers type farmhouse and outbuildings or small barns linked with brick to the side, with what looked like still having small sash windows to the lower and upper parts of the house, and an old door that spread two normal door widths. Not sure from this distance if it was a split barn door or not but was a large wide one.

"Here Taff, look see at that door there, it's been made just for you"

"What ya pointing at Wheeltrim"

"Do you think you will fit through that gap you fat git"

The comment forced a reaction from the Welshman; Taff shoved me into the others and forced them to fall over in a mess on the boggy moss filled field.

"I'm full of shit now ya wee poot"

"Jock you were full of shit before",
"Well that's just marvellous isnit. I'm here trying to direct us to the resupply point and you lot are farting about on the floor like a bunch of drunken monkeys at a tortoise only chess party. Get up"!

The other building next to the farmhouse was totally different, lying behind and appearing smaller in length but higher with at least three floors and top to bottom new plastic looking double glazing giving a fairly modern looking appearance. We walked around to the side of the old building to see more of what looked like what we thought might be a better option of finding the resup point.

"Michael have you heard anything from the Captain"?
"No last time I spoke he said just meet the contact here at these houses"
"Both houses? Or...?"
"Wies ich nicht"   (I don't know)
"Well I guess two of us should dump our kit and go knock on the door, what thinks you of that plan Herr Michael?"
"Well there is only one way to find out isn't there. Right Connal, you and meself will do that and we will signal to you if everything is in order ok"

"Sounds ok to me"

"Bonjour Monsieur"

The small and petite but absolutely stunning brunette answered the door with a welcoming smile and miniscule indiscrete wink of her hazel eyes, baffling us into embarrassment with her beauty as we were not prepared to have such a gorgeous picture framed in the double glazed doorway of this "house behind the farm".   The lady again spoke;

"Comment puis-je t'aider "

"Hello, may I help you?"

Michael looked at me in astonishment and agreement that the lady's English accent was equally as sexy as her true French spoken earlier. Michael signalled with a wave to the others waiting at the end of the path along with an open cupped hand placed upside down on top of his head to indicate "on me" or come here shnell machen (Quick style), meanwhile Taff attempted to overcome a nervous mouth problem he had getting words out correctly, and respond to the woman.

"Err, hi we are err looking for a man who might be looking for us, err to talk to about something, is there anybody here like that?"

The French woman gave an inviting hand gesture waving past her slim waistline.

"Sail vous plait venire. "   (please come in)

The French lady brought us into an immaculately clean open plan living area with leather Chesterfield type seats and mahogany framed coffee tables with what looked like crystal smoked glass that had diamond shaped emblems embedded in each corner. Next to the three post oak beamed fireplace surround was an ornate world globe made into a mini bar, opened up in half. The front half contained several glass decanters with different coloured alcohol in each. The lighting in the room was seductively dimmed and an off white colour, an almost pastel light ray shone through the decanters, a very professional aura filled the atmosphere along with a hint of fresh coffee from the kitchen. More voices came from the next room. The voices became louder and noticeably jovial and there they were. Four more beautiful young ladies appeared through an open doorway to the kitchen and came within our sight. By this time the others had all followed in and the door was shut behind us with a click.

A simultaneous quadraphonic "Bonjour gentlemen" broke the silence and made our mouths drop in awe at the pure beauty before us. Where on earth were we, what is this place, and why are we here? Connal managed to move his mouth in a nervous manner and asked the question.

"Bonjour Madamwasel, er, what is this place and er can we put our kit anywhere?"

Oui, you may put your baggage in the hallway there, and this place is a how do you say perhaps, a house of entertainment"

"A what"?

Connal made a confused dumbass face still puzzled with the French woman's answer, Taff looked at Connal also bemused by the answer.

"Bloody ell, are you two thick, what do you think it is? A home video watching house? Derrr. Look what's in front of you, entertainment house you know, for entertainment and stuff! "

Taff was spotted actually looking for a video recorder/player and matching big screen to back up my sarcastic previous statement, but eventually decided to go along with the personal entertainment theme as suggested.

"Er, we are looking for a man to speak with a contact person, maybe similar looking to us? Would you happen to have seen anyone like that? "

"You mean like Major Forrester or perhaps Captain Black? "

The French woman spoke in a more definite and positive tone, not quite as seductive as the greeting we got earlier, a more professional and business like tone, sounding more like a Personal assistant or very posh secretary.

"Marie would you please call the Major"

We placed our bergens and equipment in the hallway sort of out of the way of wandering beautiful women. In the background could be heard a very light motor running which sounded a bit like a working lift.
After all five of us looked at each other for what felt like several minutes but was actually about six seconds, a different tone of electrical motor sounded and a gap of approximately six by four feet of the bookcase on the wall opened to reveal a very relaxed and chilled Major Forrester who was donning the most obscene shell suit on the planet, an absolutely failed attempt at trendsetting or something we were sure.

"Ahhh there you are men, come on then, follow me."

We were led through the open bookcase door and into an eight man lift, steel reinforced all round with just a box on the right side containing several switches and a telecom device of some description. Taff looked behind at the kit and weapons that were left unprotected or watched, but the Major told us not to fret about that, the girls will watch them. Unbeknown to us all five girls were in a sub contracted engagement to the cause or the company or the team as it was to be known.

"Yes just in case you were wondering this is a safe house that we use quite a lot for meetings and such like, it has several disguises one of which I'm sure you have guessed. All sorts goes on here most of which you will deduce from what you are about to see."

Seconds later the lift door opened and we were led out by the Major into what can only be described as a conference room made into a briefing room, made into a mission control room/brew room. Brand new computer desks covered the shag pile carpeted floor, some were still unpacked properly and had the polystyrene attached to each corner for protection in transit. There were boxes with pictures of screens on the front and the name Hewlet Packard. The tiled walls were covered in huge geographical maps with both a grid format and contour format. Five clocks hung in a corner each showing a different time around Europe and America. Having viewed all the new furniture and technical equipment, our eyes fixated on one particular piece of equipment and one beautiful lady next to it. Yes, Carmen was here, what a sight she was, there next to the kettle making us drool at the thought of being made a cup of tea by this ex model Purdie look- a- like. Her arm movements were so angelic, she had perfected the art of standing there most adorably stirring the tea pot, what an absolute peach of a woman. Nobody dare mention who it was that put the coffee jar top back on cross threaded not whilst in the company of Carmen the great!

"Hello Boys, how are you, anybody for tea?"
"Carmen don't spoil them for god's sake, they aren't on holiday you know."

The major spoke to her as though she was Moneypenny waiting for a proposal from Bond James Bond. He told us to help Carmen dish out the drinks and make ourselves useful and open some of the unopened boxes. He introduced us to the three surveillance specialists who all had Icelandic beards and looked like a trio of Vikings from a recently docked dragon boat. Each man had an equally annoying pair of ears; they were too small, too pink, too holy, or just too full of gay rings!

"When you have finished your brew we shall get down to the job in hand, what thinks you men?"
"Er yeah why not. By the way Sir, who pays for all this stuff?"

"Stuff, what do you mean Stuff, Wheeltrim?"

"Well the house, this stuff in here, the women out front, the maps and other shit, deep pile carpets, you know, this stuff?"
"Ah well you see it's a bit clever, not sure if you will understand, but all these criminals we arrest or help the police arrest, well they have all got assets and money which they have to give us when they are in our custody,

that is, we seize by order of the government we work for at the time and keep the cash and spend it on this stuff"

"I beg your pardon Sir; you said the government we work for at the time. Do you mean we work for more than one government"?

"Ah yes well we work for at least one government, sometimes two at once, we can be sub contracted out to whoever needs us at that time. If the need for our services arises in any country and we prevent that crime, normally the crime being a kidnap because that is what we specialise in you see, then we are allowed to seize whatever assets or goods we think will aid us or be beneficial to us."

"So we don't actually get paid by the Queen then, you know the Queens shilling so to speak"

"Yes you get a minimum soldiers salary and are fully paid members of the British Army and you will get a wage slip from Her Majesty every month if I can remember to dig it out of the accounting mail box, sometimes Carmen has to remind me of this. However, you will always have access to money or any cash that you might need, do you need any?"

"Well just a few quid in our wallets might be ok Sir, what do you reckon lads?"

"Ken I've nae money to even buy a flash e whisky man"

"Right ok, Michael, give them each two large would you please"

"Naturlich"   (Of course)

"Major one last thing, do we have to grow beards and wear girly ear rings like the three stooges over there?"

"Er no, I think not, beards are ok though ear rings not so ok, well not for your job anyway. Anything else? No? Good, finish your brew then we can have a brief in the briefing room.

We all sat down in the briefing room and just for a few moments listened to Taff chunnering on about not very much, we were all immediately bored. The Major walked in the room with his "important man" clipboard and rescued us from the totally uninteresting one man conversation from the Welshman.

"Approximately fourteen miles ahead is a Farmhouse owned by an Italian businessman. This Italian has just bought a huge plot of land near the coast in South Yorkshire, stretching through to Lincolnshire. Unbeknown to him this land has extremely large amount of a special mineral embedded in it called polyhylate. This mineral is very sought after and can be used for all sorts. I don't want to give you lads a chemistry lesson now because there is a band of baddy Russians who you have already identified, who have unsuccessfully attempted to purchase the land for the purpose of selling the mineral.
We have been tasked to prevent the organised kidnap and blackmail of the Italian business man's daughter, and before you ask we have better intel than any one on the planet and that is how we know all this, and no we can't just go and arrest them because up to now they haven't committed any crime, so there you are. Your mission should you choose to accept it, which you will, is all of the above and in the process seizing as many valuable items

as possible from the said villains with limited injuries to ourselves of course. By the way chaps, we need as much slush fund items as possible as we need to survive for at least another seven months with what we have at the moment which is not a lot".

"Er Major, have we got time for some snap? We are absolutely Hank at the moment"

"Yes of course Wheeltrim, we have time for some FOOD. I will ask Carmen and the girls to rustle something up for you but it will be something light and nutritious as you have to yomp a while further to a recce point in the farm surroundings. While we are waiting I have here a map of the farm and its entry points, some are ground based, and one is below ground and two above ground to the first and top floor.

Michael, you and Wheels will observe and cover the rear entry points. Connal and Taff, you will climb to the roof access points from the outbuilding roof there and then walk along the roof to this point here and abseil over the side. There is always a window open at that level, it is a small window, but big enough to fit even grizzly soldiers like you through. Jock, you will stand fast at this point here and give sit reps to the others through this mini comms system here, which I have to warn you, is new to us and on trial. Feel free to mess about with it and practice before you set off."

"Are we all clear? Any questions? No, good. Get your scran and get ready to go, you will need full Bergen packs which will be ditched at your OP, oh and you will wear these all black combat suits, they are specifically designed to carry the necessary."

"By the way although you are supposed to be on a recce mission, we need to capture, kill or maim the perpetrators by any means necessary, that means shoot to kill when and if the need arises".

The food was brought in by the Frenchy's. Disappointingly it was some sort of dodgy fish salad, apparently useful for concentration and energy and all sorts of other things. Taff attempted to get one of the girls' phone numbers, they all had their own rooms with phones in we were told. I'm not sure how that went but the girl in question made the 'when' sign with her hands, meaning it's a no, not because she thought he was a guy with a woman in every port but probably not interested because he was welsh and couldn't understand a word what he was saying anyway.

After the food, we walked out packed with arms to the hilt as though we were going to war. We were supplied with another rifle of the very powerful fashion, a prototype L115A3 AWM with a huge scope. Michael the German said he had used them before and informed us that it usually stayed with the person who was watching over and in charge of comms, so that being Jock; he got to carry the thing all the way to the target area.

"Ken this bloody gat (Rifle) weighs a piggin ton man, av'e geet a sare heed already".

"Jock do we have to listen to your dribble all the way to this house, Taff put a crocodile on the orientation and get us the fuck out of here before we all die of boredom which can be deemed in this instance the same as listening to Jock for more than a minute".
"Well it's like this we have to go there and walk up this mountain thing there you see and then walk down the

other side and we should be able to see the farm in the distance, well maybe just maybe".

"Which of the Frenchie's do you want Michael"?

"Ya Veilliecht, I think yes the one with blonde hair and green eyes, she was looking good I think"

"Yes I think so too, however the other blonde with brown streaks and odd nails was ok as well. Do you think we will see them again?"

"Naturlich yes, they are in the team, well sort of, they run the safe houses in England and take care of other things also, things that we don't see, things that we don't want to see, you know ,,, things".

"Taff are we there yet?"

The food we had at the house was almost giving us stitches now. We did not feel sick but actually slightly high, what on earth was in that food anyway, some sort of amphetamine YES!"

The ascent up the hill should have taken it right out of us but whatever 'high protein food' it was, worked, and there was the summit. We had the mound of rocks that denoted the top of the hill in sight.

A few yards later we dumped all our bergens at the rocks to have a stretch and moan about our shoulders for a minute. Michael looked in the bino's towards the glazed Yorkshire horizon, scanning the scene for a huge farmhouse, the Consallo establishment. The bino's stopped and immediately retraced two millimetres west. Michael twiddled the refocus knob correcting the stereopsis view and his eyebrows lifted above the eyepiece in excitement and glee. The bino's were drawn down his face in slow motion revealing a joyous grin and changed to a pointed long arm indicator.

"There it is boys"
"Let's av a scan ya boxhead bampot,"

A few moments of silence ensued
"Eye it's yonder alreet Mon, have a gander at that wheeltrim ya wee basa".

Eventually we all had a turn looking through the bino's, which by this time were severely misted up and sweaty and required a clean, but the necessity to carry this out was disrupted by Taff who had spotted a small convoy of vehicles on a minor road in the distance heading towards the house. Several questions were asked between us, was it them, the Ruskies, was it just a carpet delivery man with two carpets one in each van and a gang of carpet fitters in the following car, or maybe even just random traffic.

The huge fully equipped bergens were thrown back on our ready to be rested and massaged backs, we must be carrying about seventy kilos each or what seemed like it leastways. The sniper rifle was slung low in force march order, other weapons had been strapped to the bergens with G10 mini bungees. The olive drab green equipment not exactly fashionably blended or toned to match the black urban combats we were wearing, not catwalk standard me thinks.

"Double time girls "

A slightly increased pace ensued with even more complaints from Jock about the weight we were carrying;

although we knew when we got to the target area we could dump most of the kit and proceed in skeletal kit. Michael kept a keen eye on the vehicles on the house road. They were now parked in a sort of lay by about seven hundred metres from the house and in the distance we could see several people standing next to the vehicles having a smoke. We followed a tree line down a hill in camouflage to avoid being spotted and made our way to the recce points.

Jock thanked God for allowing him to carry all that crap all that way on his back and dumped his Bergen and the rifle at his point of rest. Taff thought he could smell proper good Welsh manure; the rest of us just ignored him and prepped ourselves for the mission. The bergens were covered with foliage and left with Jock and the rifle, comms were checked and off we went.

"Ay up Michael, which one of us is on roof assault?"

"Wheels it was only half hour ago that you were told who is what and where, are you being dummkopf nochmal (thickhead again). Here grab the ropes, you can do it, I heard you were good abseiler in your past life"

"The only thing he was good at with ropes Michael mein friend is that girly game Cat's Cradle!"
"Cat's Cradle, was is das Taff?"

"Cat's cradle Michael is a game that is played with both hands normally associated with young female participants under the age of eleven. As it happens I have here in my sky rocket a spare pair of pussers shoe laces which I will now tie together in the correct length for the use of demonstrating the said game of Cat's Cradle as performed by Wheeltrim."

"Oh my god, are you really putting your hands in your pocket and actually wasting time and energy whilst navigating us around this field towards the target house carrying all that shit, weapons, ammo, night vision stuff, hip flask and all, Taff ?"

"Well you did ask what it is didn't you boyo."

"Taff shittin ell, we are about to put the frighteners on Boris and the bananas and you are fannying around with a piece of string wrapped around your hands doing a very bad job of what I can do better, give that string here you nob!"

I very quickly went through the Cat's Cradle using the joined up olive drab G10 laces correctly wrapping fingers around each other twisting and turning wrists creating a wizardry of webbed patterns beyond recognition to the naked eye, or at least to the other who wouldn't know that I had actually slipped up slightly but miraculously recovered to end the demo with the reverse move to back in the original starting place.

"There you go!"
"Congratulations you big wet lettuce, now can we get on with the task in hand, if you get my drift"

After twenty minutes Michael was weighing up the situation in front, and just about to dish out the 'we will split up now and go to our respective points' order and then turned around to speak and viewed three men stood away from the wind each with their left hand on their hips, right hand holding something in front. Ah yes the old synchronised pissing routine, should have expected that. Doh!

"Ok, finished?,   So Taff,   you and I will take position to the rear, then that will leave yourself Wheels and Connal to cover roof and top floor points, there is a huge old fashioned drainpipe to the rear of the adjoining building you can use to gain access to the high roof,   maintain radio silence unless anything urgent arises. You have six flash bangs each, that should be plenty, and we are not expecting any action for a few hours so make sure you are in position in good time. Go."

Michael did radio checks with Jock by calling him a fat useless pisshead, to see if he was still awake and could hear clearly, the words came back in reply, "shut it ya wee poof" proved that everything was good with comms. Connal and I made camouflaged haste to the rear of the adjoining outbuilding   with a view to find the said drainpipe,   climb it and jump across to the actual farmhouse from which we would then abseil into the window, and gain access to the house, rescue everybody, hand them over to the police,   then home for tea and medals, hoorah !!!

"Here Connal grab hold of that rope while I shimmy up this old pipe will ya matey"
"Eye pal "
I ascended up the old rickety drainpipe grabbing hold of each rusty round steel bracket, wrapping my legs around the eroded discoloured circular tubing, a certain aroma filled the area between my face and the pipe, a mixture

of rotting metal, age old moss and sewer all mixed up, a real good barbeque sauce smell.

I was half way up the pipe when I realised something, something ridiculous, something very stupid, bugger, the rope! Why did I not bring it up with me so I could pull up the kit? Shit, Bugger.

"Paddy! See if you can't throw that rope up ere where I can catch it, I need it up here, Derr."

"Well I was going to say why didn't you take it up with you then you could pull up all the kit?"

"But you didn't "

"No"

"Just chuck it here bloody ell, give a boy a man's job or what?"

On the seventh attempt I managed to catch a flying carabiner with my right index finger and just about balance myself to retain the rope and stop it from being launched again. My grip on the slippy moss needed some readjustment, which required a leg movement and certain balancing act reminiscent of a pole dancer. My left leg in a forty degree angle left of the pipe, and my right arm seventy degrees to the right, Rudolf Nureyev would be proud. The carabiner now securely clipped to my belt buckle, I continued up and up. My German para combat boots slipping on the brown and green fungi growing on the inside towards the insecure securing screws, only another four pipe brackets to go and I was there. Slowly but surely the heavy kit was pulled and heaved up the side of the wall dragging along a heap load of unwanted creatures and a rapid response to duck down out of sight was required as a farmer or horse hand walked close by. We continued and Connal proceeded to climb and join me

on the roof. We walked over the slightly pitched roof and came across the gap that was the way to our entry point.
"Connal have you seen that whopping great big gap we have to jump. Piggin ell man.!"
"Eye it's a wee bit large man isnnit"

We both took a moment to view the mission in front of us, and also see what other items around us could be used in Krypton factor style to get us across the whopping great gap from one building to the other. Maybe we could use the pussers climbing rope we were issued and fashion a rope bridge and dangle in true Marine rope bridge crossing order.

"See anything Connal?"
"Nah, not really. Although, what are those two bits of wood protruding up over the roof there?"

I was a little puzzled as to how two small pieces of wood at the end of the roof would help us get across to the other side. Out of pure curiosity I followed Connal to the end of the roof to pick up the pieces of wood and await his explanation. We took care in scaling over the roof, approached the end and looked over the top, and there it was; a huge four piece ladder erected from the floor up.

"Shit you mean to say we have struggled with the wall ascent trying to grip a manky old mushroom and biddy infested drainpipe, when there is a perfectly serviceable ladder here Shit"
"Never mind that now here grab the bloody thing and pull up, we can use it as a bridge".
"Good thinking Batman"

The ladder weighed an absolute ton, probably made of some cedar or ash wood or something well heavy, the ladder crept up the wall slowly but surely, each side gradually chipping away at the tiles on the roof, loosening and dislodging them away from their age old fixings. Our triceps were burning by now but only about three foot to go, the weight of the ladder in its upright position was forcing it to unbalance and tipple to one side and forced us to readjust our stance.

"Connal get to the other side of the ladder I reckon I can support it here, we can't let it crash onto the roof or it will probably put a hole in it".
"Give us a min"
"Yeah well put a crocodile on it there is a wind brewing".

I supported the ladder with great discomfort and prevented it from falling over while Connal took what seemed like three hours to crawl about sixteen and a half feet over the roof. The ladder was carried on our shoulders to the point of crossing where we took a break to wipe the sweat from our brows and massage our extremely tired arms, and contemplated the next task. We knew the ladder had to be stood up again to then drop it onto the next roof, and then it was just a matter of getting across on all fours.

Below us in between the buildings was a small man made river that looked like it wasn't very deep, probably used for powering a hydro generator somewhere in another building, but caused an extra obstruction and didn't help our cause, we assessed the situation and realised the time was cracking on we had to get it done sharpish.

Connal stood up ready but paused for a second and touched his ear attempting to force his comms earpiece in further, a message came through but was not heard. Connal touched the mouthpiece microphone stick which was protruding from under his black cotton bob hat which doubled as a balaclava when needed.

"Jock did you speak?"

"Eye, are you in position yet ya wee poof?"

"Er no, had a problem but we are adapting, improvising and overcoming the situation, why what's up?"

"Nothing, just a wee bit scunnerred (bored) here on ma jacksie "

Over the comms we heard Michael the German say "halten die Klappen sofort, or words to the effect of shut your face immediately and maintain radio silence.
 Oh dear!

"Here Connal grab that rope and lets wrap it around a ladder rung and throw it over the gap, if we get it high enough it should just drop down while we hold and lower one end, easy peasy!"

"Oh Yeah, craic - on Wheels"

The ladder all of a sudden and quite miraculously decided to increase in size and weight and was so much more difficult to move, perhaps it was our arms even more tired than before, the cramp now taking major effect, and every limb movement seemed to exacerbate the pain and soreness. The ladder was eventually erected straight up and balanced on the edge of the roof waiting to be lowered under control by two sets of arms, one taking a secure grip to one end of the rope.

"Nice and easy does it Connal man, slowly slowly catchy monkey, you know the score."
"Me soddin arms are killin man"
"Nearly there"

Approximately six foot from touching the roof two muffled voices screamed very quietly like under our breath so nobody could hear, the ladder increased in speed, we couldn't hold it anymore. The bang on the opposite roof wasn't actually that loud, however did shatter a few tiles and sent them tumbling to the floor. We looked at the makeshift bridge in jubilation and congratulated ourselves with a satisfying nod; Connal punched me in the arm and said nice one mucker, then caressed his arm that he punched me with as it hurt him more that it hurt me.

"Right let's get ourselves and the kit across there and get into position me old china"

Taff and Michael were seated in position in a small barn amongst some hay bales with a very clear view of the front and side door to the main building, ready and waiting for further instructions or action to react to. Taff looked around his feet and legs area puzzled as to what sort of cow shit was strattled across the lower part of his body, which came about when he slipped whilst jumping across a small obstacle and ended up knee high in dung. Michael strained to keep a straight face but did question Taff as to why he did not know what sort of cow left the shit in that place to which he had landed.

With everyone in position, waiting in anticipation, after two hours of nothing we were getting restless, no messages, no nothing from anywhere, was this thing happening or not.

"Here Connal sort this rope out with the crabs (carabiner) and figure of eight so we are ready to abseil into oblivion, I take it you have remembered what to do, and how to do it?"

"Yes of course ya clown I know what to do."

"Ok then "

Our banter was interrupted by a very short message from Michael the German which said, "Be ready look in, vehicles on the way."

"Connal pas me that gat (assault rifle) is it loaded? "
"Yeah safety on"
"Have you got those flash bangs "
"Yeah stop stressing "

We gently lowered the two ropes down the side of the building aiming them on either side of the window we were supposed to enter. The window looked very small from up here but was apparently big enough because Major Forrester said it was.

He did have access to the building plan with all the measurements and had the three stooges with beards look at it in detail, so it must be right. We looked at each other in anticipation and excitement, an element of fright and adrenalin rushed through our veins, prompting us to check our equipment, all tight and secure on our black outfits, nothing dangling or causing obstruction, no vision or hearing impediment that would hamper the speedy descent we were about to undertake.

Taff and Michael were just about getting comfortable and almost asleep when the comms radio blurted out a message, it was the Captain, informing us that there might be nothing happening for a while as the person who the Russians needed was only just landing at Leeds Bradford and would be a while before he was in the area, but keep alert and do not fall asleep.

In the Farmhouse the Consallo family were waiting patiently for a call from Michael who would be ringing from the airport to ask if the driver had set off to collect him. Alana the daughter was skipping and happily milling about in anticipation on the return of her Father, who had promised to take her with him next time. Mrs Consallo was busy in the kitchen making a Chicken Cacciatori for the sit down meal, tidying up as she went along.

A sharp head movement towards the telephone was the reaction to the old fashioned ring tone to which Alana sprinted to beat her Mum to pick up the receiver. During the time that Alana talked to her Father a lone van appeared on the road leading up to the drive to the farm. Jock was the first to notice and warned us on the comms, "one driver in the seat, plain unmarked white van on its way in" he said, "looks like he is on his own, could be a scout don't know might be some Russian dude." Jock aimed his telescopic sight at the van, readjusting the camouflage which was covering the end and kept springing back over the eyepiece requiring one of the G10 elastic scrim bands to be moved over a little. How very annoying, a little more preparation prevents piss poor performance yup!

"What's happenin Jock, who is that"?

"I'm just on it now scoping the swinehund"

"Yeah well don't be shy; if he gives any sign just shoot the cunt".

"Eye, just got my mince pies on him now"

Michael was listening in the background.

"What is mince pies?"

"Ken ya wee poof! Eye's innit derrr. I reckon he is just a scout giving the place a recce, I'm watching very carefully, this scope is the bollocks man, it's like fifty times bigger already, I can see his tramp stamps on his neck."

Michaels head popped up after hearing this as he knew one of the Russian villains had a tattoo on his neck but could not remember what it was, he was sure it was some sort of animal or snake or serpent of some description, with teeth and other venom spurting antenna protruding from its frontal orifice.

"Jock this is very important yetz, is the tattoo some sort of reptile "

"Dinni Ken but, the wearer of the tatt is a definitely a slimy fucker".
"Is it a snake, can you see "?

Jock took a moment to readjust the micro adjuster on the scope and zoomed in even more and more, one or two seconds to think of the picture in front of him, now as clear as day.

"Eye Michael, it's a frog thing"

"Do you mean a lizard Jock"?

"Eye ken, that's what I said a lizard, and it is red"

"Schelsse, das Ist one of the Kolorovs. Ok we are on! What's he doing now Jock?"

"Just walking back to his van and picking his nose!"

"Ok then, look in"

The ruskie got back in the van and drove back towards whence he came at slightly more speed than on the way in, spinning a few of the lightly peppered paving stones with the tyres. The van vanished through the tunnel of trees that overhung the exit road to the farmhouse to no doubt report back to his crew.

A further hour passed and dusk was appearing rapidly, light was dimming and the night dew rattled into Jocks black combat assault suit as he lay there in waiting eating a Hershey bar from his American ration pack while occasionally casting an eye over the scope to see if he could see his mates in the small outhouse, he could see Wheeltrim and Connal on the roof who waved in boredom and gave the finger.

Michael Consallo was in the car and on his way back home, the journey was just less than twenty miles but took just over a half hour, most of the roads were small A roads and had slow tractors transporting their farming things and cattle here and there. His family visit, his business meetings and money raising complete, Michael looked forward to spending time with his wife and watch his daughter riding the horses. He missed the late night brandy on the veranda overlooking the lodge, reminding him of the undulating Italian landscape with lakes dotted around.

It was time. The convoy of vans and cars started their engines and set off towards the farmhouse. In slow order keeping equal distance from each other, uniformly and correctly the four vehicles made tracks all looking professional and as though this was a regular occurrence. The small van in front had been before and the security guard let him in without question. He was about to slow down the second van using the European hand signal for stop, a hand placed up in front of the moving vehicle and a few steps towards it, but the second van window was already half way down and a machine pistol silencer protruded from the glass. Before the guard could react three futting noises and a thump threw him backwards awkwardly and his knees buckled under the pain and sudden loss of feeling in his legs. As the van drove past another two shots rained on the guards head, his arms and head lay awkwardly in a star shape. His body holed with bullets, blood poured onto the gravel floor, tinting the grey finish a light crimson colour. Several after death body jerks rustled the ground until the silent corpse was dragged to a nearby tree by the Russian with the frog on his neck.

The four vehicles drove around the back of the house and parked up next to the outhouses where Michael and Taff were in hiding. Three villains quickly got out of each vehicle, and placed weapons of mass destruction about their torsos. The tallest one seemed to be in charge as he was pointing to each man to cover each door and the remaining men made their way to the front door, and surprisingly, politely knocked.

Mrs Consallo didn't get chance to see who it was as she opened the door. The door was barged open by the big Russian and hit the unsuspecting woman and threw her rearwards to the floor. The deep pile welcome rug rippled under her body and the Russian seized the opportunity to grab the end of the rug and roll the struggling woman in the makeshift blanket forcing her arms inside. He thrust his knees against the Italian material and delved into his Crombie pocket to get tape. Alana had followed her mother into the entrance hallway and started screaming at the sight before her. "Mama Mama" she cried while looking where she could get help, but no one was there. The driver was picking up Daddy, and the security guard was at the gate, dead! Tears streamed down her face as Mrs Consallo's head turned from left to right in horror and desperation in an attempt to plead with the assailants to spare her.

"Boris get her "

The girl turned about and tried to run but it was too late, one of the three Russians was already behind her and grabbed her, his arms around her slim body. Gripping her tightly he picked her up and threw her across his shoulder. With one arm still free the Russian withdrew a huge Bowie style knife from his pocket and pointed it at the girls face in an attempt to stop her screaming and install terror and fear in her mind. The girl was thrown into a chair and with arms forced rearwards behind the wooden slats, plastic tie wraps restrained her hands and more tape was used to silence her.

The noise of the assault through the door and the screams alerted Taff and Michael, Connal and I were still on the roof and could hear but not see what was happening inside, but we could see the Russians guarding the outside and watch the way in and out.

Michael the German was already plotting a response and very quickly assessed the situation.

"Jock can you see what's going on, can you see any targets, do you have a clear shot anywhere?"
"Eye, I can see four targets, two at the blue barn door near you and another two east of you near the van. I can also see in the house through the patio windows, they have I think two hostages tied up"
"Ok listen in, Connal and Wheetrim, on three you get yourselves down the ropes and into the house through that window. Jock, you take out the tall one of the Russians at the blue door and Taff give the small one lead in the head".

"Three, two, one".

Taff pointed his silenced pistol at the small Russian and squeezed the trigger, two bullets phutted and projected through the slat in the barn and embedded themselves in the Russians head, exploding brain matter in random multiple directions. In a simultaneous milli second the tall Russians head was jetopulted backwards and the g-force of the movement forced him into a backward somersault throwing his legs up into the air and then landing uncomfortably upside down on what was left of his head. A deep bone crack could be heard, his neck broke and forehead shattered, he was dead, and with no movement from his mate we were to presume him dead also.

We thrust ourselves out the barn door and made our way to the other two Russians who we could see had heard some disturbance and were throwing their fags moving towards the noise. Jock fired again, a moving target shot, a moment of luck perhaps but one of the Russians was floored with a shot to the abdomen, blood and guts splattered across the ground and covered his mate with fragments of yellow, red and white intestines. The other Russian turned and looked in horror at the mess that was his comrade. He roared in anger, and adrenalin pushed him to point his weapon at us, but he was too late. Michael already had a commando throwing knife at the ready and the knife was already airborne flying into the Russians neck. He dropped his weapon and used both hands to grasp the wound, pulling the knife out of his neck in the hope it would help, but Michael had aimed the knife perfectly, piercing a main artery. An arterial spray jettisoned into the air creating a red vision in front of us. The Russians head twisted and kinked to the right and the eyes followed the colour of the spray too. His head was blown, brain could not cope with the lack of blood and oxygen, and he fainted dead on the floor.

"Taff come on, he's well gone let's get in the house"

"Wheels can you hear me?"

"Yeah"

"Get yourselves down those ropes and in to clear the rooms, go"

"Roger that"

"C'mon Connal "

Connal went over the roof first grabbing his figure of eight eyelet and very quickly slid down the wall making it look so easy. Within seconds he was pushing himself against the wall to get a good position to kick in the window, but he stopped himself on his final swing and came to a stop right in front of the glass, bugger, it was a sash window set up. It would be very difficult to kick in the glass with the horizontal slats. It would be a matter of gentle persuasion he thought. He reached behind and into a pouch/scabbard and brought forward a bayonet shaped knife which looked more like a sword of mass destruction. Connal forced the razor sharp implement into the rotting paint flaked Accoya wood strip and moved the blade slightly to the left to release the twist action lock, lifted the wood strip with his other hand and replaced the knife. He showed me the thumbs up to which I reciprocated, he was in.

I immediately threw myself over the top, left hand operating the eyelet, right hand grabbing the wall for support. On my descent towards the window my hand struck something incredibly sharp on the wall and it pierced it straight through. I could see an old nail protruding out of my hand which was holding against the wall, a biting excruciating pain rocketed through my arm making me grab hold on the rope to stop the descent. Shit, I was stuck. How on earth was I to get out of this one, my left hand stuck on the figure of eight. If I let go, the weight of my body would sink and probably rip my hand off the nail, it was in deep and it was pointing upwards and so a bit difficult to just remove my hand and carry on.

Connal must have realised that I wasn't directly behind him, came back and poked his head through the window and asked what I was doing.

"Wheels what are you doing"

"I'm stuck, in severe pain but still alive! Carry on without me."

Connal looked behind him for something long. He grabbed a brush from the corner of the room, removed his first aid kit and with the Sellotape included in the kit he taped a morphine tablet lightly to the end of the stick and passed it up to me. I bit off the pill and spat out the remnants of the sticky tape,

"Cheers r kid. Now bog off and sort the job out",

Connal continued on his mission and left me in a crucifixion position on the wall just above the window.

The Russians heard the commotion and sent two operatives out to see what was going on. One went up the stairs, the other through the kitchen to the back door. He opened the huge back door and was thrown several feet backwards with blood shooting out of his back which splattered all over the black and white chequered kitchen tiles and units. Taff and Michael reloaded both their assault rifles and ran in to the house, flash bangs in hand they approached the front room where the remaining two Russians held the two hostages seated, tied up and gagged.

Connal was upstairs and having cleared several rooms was now on the landing moving towards the stairs when he saw the Russian on the second flight. He lifted and aimed at the same time as the Russian, nine shots were fired, only one by Connal. Connal's shot hit first, the Russian fell backwards and in a last moment of life squeezed his trigger and shot eight rounds into mid-air. One of the bullets ricocheted off the top rail banister ball brass handle and landed in Connal's leg prompting him to lift his leg in pain and lose his balance. He grabbed his wound in an attempt to stop the bleeding. The bullet didn't go through, it was lodged in his shin, he could see the spent round through the fleshy part of his leg. He had left the first aid kit below the window just in case I managed to get in somehow and needed another morphine tablet. Connal attempted to remove his belt with the idea to compress the wound with the belt which would hopefully stop the bleeding. Each time he removed his hand to unbuckle the belt, blood poured out of his leg. He had to manage the job with one hand which required a different position putting him in more pain; the bullet must have touched a nerve.

Taff and Michael walked gingerly in the direction of the front room; an uncanny silence came about all of a sudden, what was going on? Their eyes were scanning left and right, but nothing, were they too late, had they vanished all of a sudden? No, Jock would have seen them and said summat on the intercom.

"Aha, there you is"

Taff and Michael walked in and saw both Russians smiling with an eerie confidence. One of the Russians had a bread knife across the young girl's neck that had her tears dripping off it onto her blouse. A speckle of blood creeped down from below the blade, her skin had only just been creased.
The other Russian stood over the Mother with a pistol casually pointed at her neck, not really thinking that we would react. His slackness showed and maybe just maybe we could get a shot at at least one of them, daughter first was our primary thought.

"You will not walk any closer, or we do some damage, ya?"

Taff and Michael were aiming at both Russians with their Hecks. A milli second later, Jock spoke through the mike,

"I have a clear shot at the Russian nod your head if you want and when you want me to take it."

Taff aimed his weapon at the Russian on the left and Michael the one on the right, they had both heard Jock through the intercom and then Michael slowly moved his weapon to aim at the same Russian as Taff. Taff knew what was coming. Michael nodded his head, the first sound that was heard was the glass double glazing shatter with the rifled projectile still spinning through the air and directly into the skull of the big Ruski. Simultaneously, six rounds were fired into the head of the other Russian, exploding his teeth and other matter across the room and covering the Mother in red sticky blood. That was it, job done!

We quickly set about calming the hostages down and untying them from their bindings as though it was natural to do so. Jock came racing through the door with rifle aimed in hand looking a bit sweaty from his run down the hill he asked.
"Everyone ok?"
"Don't think so Jock, haven't seen Wheels or Connal "
Connal had heard the question as he was now half way down the staircase.
"I'm up here, give me a bandage and go and sort Wheels out, he is half way up the wall at the back with something sharp sticking out of his hand"
Michael instructed Taff and Jock to go sort out Wheeltrim the nob while he calmed and questioned the two female hostages.

Jock walked around the back of the house with Taff trying to figure out which wall Connal was on about, they should just look for the one with the dangly person attached to the side.

"Wheels ya wee poof, what the fuck are you doing up there"

"Ah Jock, Taff, get the ladders from up yonder and get me down and get me another morphine tablet and put a crocodile on it! My hand is killing me"

Taff raced off to get the ladders while Jock continued to take the piss with a relentless onslaught of neverendingness. Finally, the ladders were thrown against the wall and Taff climbed up to lift my hand off the rusty nail and pull me on to the rungs of the ladder, down we went at last.

We talked to the two women whilst they made us all a brew. We were eternally grateful even though the tea bags were the type that had a string attached to them and just looked silly and very difficult to stir the right amount of times clockwise and anti-clockwise without the string getting twisted around the spoon. Still, a cup of tea is a cup tea.

Our drink was interrupted by the sound of two engines, one a very quiet motor car engine which was pulling on the drive. This car was driven by a professional driver. We could tell because he passed the door first time without stopping just in case something was wrong, his suspicions aroused by the absence of a guard on the gate. The car pulled over and the driver got out and Mrs Consallo signalled to him everything was ok. Michael Consallo got out and ran to his wife, as they embraced, Alana the daughter ran over to join them.

The other engine noise to be heard was the Huey landing in the horse field with the Captain and the Major onboard plus the three stooges with Icelandic beards and Carmen the beauty in the back seats. They had all come to approve of the successful mission it seemed.

The Major and the Captain got out and the rest followed

"Right chaps well done. If you go over to Carmen at the Huey she will bandage up any wounds. I will take over here Michael thank you, I need to ask Mr Consallo a few questions, and the three beards will tidy up and remove all villains' vehicles for our possession.

We picked up our kit and walked wearily over to the chopper, weapons slung over our arms and belts dangling from wounds, bags adrift our bodies. The evening moon shone in front of us creating a shadow that resembled five walking trees off into the distance, although the distance was only about fifty feet it seemed to take ages to get there.

The three beards finished the clean-up and the gaffers finished talking to the owners telling them that the police would arrive soon and to tell them that Sok-7 had been and gone.

Our dressings were of hospital standard as was the morphine; even the people who were not injured had some. We were a little spaced to understand what the Majors debrief contained but it was basically saying we have one day to chill out then we are to get ourselves to Brize Norton for a flight to USA Virginia, Langley, our spy training starts, two months of sneaky beaky training

Yippee.

The End.

Printed in Great Britain
by Amazon